# FIRE AND ICE

(HEARTS ON FIRE, BOOK 2)

ROBIN BRANDE

RYER PUBLISHING

**FIRE AND ICE**
**(Hearts on Fire, Book 2)**
**By Robin Brande**

Published by Ryer Publishing
www.ryerpublishing.com

Cover photos Dreamstime.com
Cover design by Robin Ludwig Design, Inc.
www.gobookcoverdesign.com
ISBN: 978-1-952383-36-6

❀ Created with Vellum

# ALSO BY ROBIN BRANDE

**Romance**

*Love Proof*

*Freefall*

*Heart of Ice*

*Fire and Ice*


**Winnie-Parsons-Mysteries**

*The Genius Track*

*A Man of Appetites*

*A Drop of Sweat*

*The Long Gray Hook*

*The Slip of a Rib*


**Dove Season-Series**

*Dove Season*

*Finder*

*Seeker*

*Believer*


**Bradamante-Saga**

*Book of Earth*

*Book of Water*

## Young-Adult

*Evolution, Me & Other Freaks of Nature*

*Fat Cat*

*Doggirl*

*Replay*

## Parallelogram-Series

*Into the Parallel*

*Caught in the Parallel*

*Seize the Parallel*

*Beyond the Parallel*

## Collections

*The Love of a Good Dog*

*Mountain Tough*

## Self-Help

*What If You're Doing It Right?*

*What If You're Doing It Right? For Teens*

# FIRE AND ICE

1

---

"You think I look hot in my tuxedo," Thorsten said.

The truth was, Shannon had been thinking exactly that. Thorsten's jacket hugged his wide shoulders and trim athletic torso perfectly. His work as a kayaking and wilderness guide had sculpted his body into the proportions Shannon liked. His crisp white shirt and black tie drew attention to the square jaw above it, the full, upcurved lips, the careless tousle of wavy brown hair, his soft blue eyes.

*Enjoy the scenery*, Shannon reminded herself, *but that's as far as it goes.*

She shrugged. "Even Quasimodo looked good in a tux."

"You think I don't know who that is."

"I'm hoping you do."

Thorsten smiled. He leaned casually against the wall of the banquet hall and handed Shannon a glass of wine. "*Skál,*" he said, clinking his own glass against hers.

"Scowl," Shannon repeated. If she hadn't heard Thorsten

give the Icelandic cheer several times at the rehearsal dinner the night before, she might have thought he was commenting on her expression.

They had been bantering like this since the rehearsal dinner, Shannon always just a step ahead of Thorsten's flirtation. He was charming and not hard to look at, and that was the problem. She had seen plenty of both in recent times and had lost her taste for it. Charming men required extra precautions. Inevitably flirtation led to passion led to discovery, then straight to disappointment. She had yet to meet a man who lived up to his own hype.

She had decided on the plane down to Arizona that what she needed in her life instead was a dog. Or a fish—something simple that didn't ask much more than to be fed and noticed. A plant might do. She would have to look into it when she returned home from her cousin's wedding.

"You look hot, too," Thorsten told her.

"Thanks, but we don't really say 'hot' here once we're over thirty."

"I still think you're hot. You smell nice, too."

"It's soap."

"Soap. Hmm. I'll try that. Our people have always used whale blubber."

She had to admire Thorsten's ability to keep up with her —especially considering English was his second language. Shannon had met plenty of American men who would have given up the chase by now, realizing she presented too much of a challenge. It was why she dated fellow attorneys more than men with any other occupation—she liked the mental stimulation offered by a man who could give as good as he got. But right now she wasn't looking for any kind of stimulation. She just wanted a week of relaxation with her family.

Still, she found herself looking forward to her interactions with the groom's brother. Whenever Thorsten approached she braced for another volley. She liked his quick humor. She liked the sound of his voice. His accent was subtle and melodic—the round vowels, the soft roll of his r's. At the rehearsal dinner the night before she eavesdropped as Thorsten and his brother Kjartan conversed in Icelandic. She liked listening to the lilt of it, to the rhythm and cadence of the ancient Viking tongue.

There was no harm in simply talking to him, Shannon rationalized. She could spar with Thorsten without worrying what it might lead to. After the wedding they would never see each other again. Thorsten would return to Iceland, Shannon to Minneapolis—it was a no-risk game as long as she stayed on her side of the boundary and he stayed on his. And she meant to enforce that line.

Shannon took a sip of wine and surveyed the room. Annie and Kjartan were still trapped near the entrance, unable to move past the throng of well-wishers. Shannon's brothers had already made it to the bar, and now hovered near the buffet table. About fifty other guests roamed the banquet hall. The DJ warmed up with slow, quiet love songs.

Shannon leaned against the wall and glanced at Thorsten from the corner of her eye. "That was a nice thing you said about your brother during the ceremony."

Thorsten shrugged. "I stole it from a book."

"What was the part you said in Icelandic?"

"It's an old Viking toast: Hurry your sheep to your own pasture."

"That sounds nice. What does it mean?"

"It means your wife has two large brothers—don't let them see you messing around."

"What does it really mean?"

"Have a happy marriage. Make a happy home."

Shannon peered at him skeptically. "Never mind. I'll ask Kjartan."

"Don't you trust me?"

"Not so far."

The crowd around Annie and Kjartan had dispersed by now, freeing the newlyweds to aim for the buffet.

Shannon pushed away from the wall. "Time to go hug my cousin."

Thorsten caught her arm. "You're not dancing with anyone but me tonight. Promise."

Shannon tried to ignore the feeling that shot through her, just from that light contact. "Sorry, it doesn't work that way." She loosened his hand.

"It's just you and me from now on, baby. No one loves you the way I do."

Shannon cocked an eyebrow. "Where did you learn your English—from old gangster movies?"

"I watch American TV all the time—lawyer shows, police shows, hospital shows. I know all the latest words."

"Oh, yeah? Like what?"

"Get me 10 cc's of saline—stat!"

"Very good. And useful, in case someone here needs a pretend doctor."

"I read American books, too. I like to keep up on how to seduce American women."

"Oh, is that what you're doing?" Shannon scanned the women at the reception. "Which one are you going to seduce?"

Thorsten slipped his arm around her waist. He leaned toward her and whispered, "Don't pretend you don't like me. I know you do."

His warm breath on her ear, his confident banter, the feeling of his hip against hers and his arm draped so casually around her waist—she was surprised by how much it flustered her. *Steady, girl. You're just out of practice.*

"I guess I haven't watched enough TV lately," she answered. "I didn't know this was how it's done. Does this work on Icelandic women, too?"

"Oh, no. I'd use a totally different method if you were from Iceland. I wouldn't be so subtle."

"Subtle, huh? Yeah, you're certainly that."

"So what about it—you and me? Forever?"

She stepped out of his embrace and patted his chest. "I'll think it over. Let me see what other offers I get tonight."

His smile was dangerously close to irresistible. "I know you'll be back. Anyone can see we're perfect for each other."

Shannon shook her head. "You're nothing like your brother."

"And you're nothing like your cousin." Thorsten leaned toward her and whispered conspiratorially. "Kjartan wouldn't know what to do with a woman like you. I know exactly what you want."

"Oh, yeah? Two more weeks of vacation and a new pair of skis? Who told you?"

Thorsten grinned. "I can wait longer than you can, sugarplum. I'm used to long cold winters. I'll be back for our first dance."

Thorsten drifted casually into the crowd before Shannon could come up with the snappy retort that she knew was trapped somewhere there in the back of her throat.

*Sugarplum? Give me a break.*

Still, she couldn't deny that warm flush on her cheeks. She was too jaded to blush anymore, but there it was. *Snap out of it.*

The only remedy was to keep her distance. She angled toward Annie, but found her already engulfed in another ring of guests. Shannon searched for her brothers and found them at the far end of the room. She headed for the comfort of family.

But Thorsten beat her to them. Shannon veered off, searching for her mother, an acquaintance—anyone.

"Hey, Shan!" her brother Chris called. Reluctantly Shannon turned. He waved her over. She shook her head and pointed toward the bar. "Okay," Chris said, "but come right back."

*Great.* Shannon ditched the wine glass and switched to something more her taste—a dark Mexican beer with a chunk of lime floating on top. She took her time getting back. Thorsten was still there.

Shannon took a sip from the bottle and did her best to focus on her brothers. "What's up?"

"Will had a great idea."

"That's new." She could hear the change in her voice. It seemed to have dropped an octave, the way it did whenever she talked to opposing counsel on the phone. She was in control again. No more girlish reactions.

"Thorsten's going to take Will's place on our backpacking trip."

She didn't realize she was staring at Thorsten until he turned and locked eyes with her. He smiled innocently. Shannon looked away and took another sip of beer while she devised a compelling argument against the plan.

"Hmm," she stalled. "Um, I don't know..."

*Wipe that grin off your face, Thorsten. No way you're going.*

"I brought all that gear," Will explained. "Thorsten might as well use it."

What had originally been planned as a backpacking trip for Shannon and all three of her brothers was now a brother short. Will had gotten a call from his boss the night before, asking him to come back for an emergency meeting of the engineering team on Monday.

Shannon shrugged apologetically. "Sorry, but I don't think it's a good idea."

"Why not?" her youngest brother Michael challenged.

"It's a pretty advanced hike."

"I think he can handle it, Shan. It's his job."

She tried again. "It's a family trip."

"He's family now," Michael pointed out. "We're cousins-in-law."

"Look, Thorsten, no offense," Shannon said, "but this is a time for my brothers and me to be together. You understand."

"Sure." He gazed at her with the unmistakable confidence of a man who knew he would win in the end.

"Sorry, B.C.," Michael said with finality, "he's going."

"B.C.?" Thorsten asked. "What's that?"

"Nothing," Shannon and her brothers answered in unison. *Thank goodness for that,* she thought. *They haven't turned on me completely.*

But she wasn't finished yet. "There are snakes out there, Thorsten—rattlers. There's scorpions, and—"

"Giants and ogres and elves," Thorsten replied. "We have those, too. Don't worry—I'll be fine. I'd love to go. I've always wanted to backpack in America."

"Good," Michael said, "it's settled."

Shannon fumbled. "It's not settled—"

"What's the problem?" Chris asked her. "Don't you like Thorsten?"

Shannon favored her oldest brother with a deadly glare. "Of course I like him," she answered with false sweetness. "Who wouldn't?"

She could feel Thorsten's eyes. She would not look his way.

"Okay," Chris said. "Good." He turned to Thorsten. "We'll look at Will's gear tomorrow morning. I'm sure his pack'll fit you."

"He doesn't have boots," Shannon tried, but her heart was no longer in it. She knew she had been bested, but her training as a litigator taught her to keep fighting no matter how long the odds.

"I do, actually," Thorsten answered. "I hoped to do some hiking when I was here."

"Great," Shannon mumbled. The rest of the plans filtered in and out of her ears as she stood there finishing her beer. *Four days of concentrated Thorsten. So much for relaxing with the boys and enjoying nature.*

Eventually the conversation turned to other topics. Shannon felt a touch at her elbow. Thorsten motioned for her to follow him out of earshot of her brothers. "If you really don't want me to go..."

"It's fine," she answered in a tone intended to convey just the opposite. "Of course you can come." Her voice was deep again, stiff. She was all business.

Thorsten regarded her silently for a moment, then said, "Okay, good. Sounds like fun."

Shannon mumbled some excuse and escaped in search of Annie. She lingered near the bride waiting for the chance to speak in private.

"It's a conspiracy," Shannon said when they were alone. "Somehow Thorsten convinced my brothers to let him come on our backpacking trip. You need to do something. Doesn't Thorsten have to stay here and help you guys pack up the house?"

Annie smiled sympathetically. "Sorry, but the truth is I'm glad he's going. I wasn't sure how we were going to entertain him this week. We're going to be pretty busy."

"Look," Shannon said, "I have a problem with the guy, okay? I'll admit it—he's a little...too cute for me."

"You mean you like him?"

"No." She pointed sternly at Annie's smile. "*No.* But he's trying something with me, and I don't really feel like dealing with it."

"Trying what?"

"Trying to pull off another Icelandic seduction, like Kjartan did with you."

Annie laughed. "Believe me, Kjartan wasn't trying—it just happened."

"Yeah, well Thorsten is working very hard on the project." Shannon shook her head wearily. "I just don't have the energy for it right now."

"You mean to resist him?" Annie asked, "or to take him up on it?"


THORSTEN STUDIED the cousins from across the room. Superficially they were similar: Both were 32, both had dark brown hair, gray-green eyes, and short, shapely bodies. But the similarities ended there.

Annie was open, forthright, easy to know. No other woman could have coaxed Thorsten's brother Kjartan out of his retirement from love. Annie's warmth and romantic view of the world had proven to be just the cure Kjartan needed.

Shannon was a different woman entirely—more guarded. She was competitive—he could see that from their conversations, the way she never wanted to give him the last word. She looked sturdier, more athletic than her cousin. Shannon's short, sleeveless blue dress showcased both her feminine curves and the round, sexy muscles of her shoulders and calves. She looked fit, rather than skinny. When he wrapped his arm around her waist he felt real flesh, not the unappealing boniness of a woman obsessed with her weight.

In fact, he had rarely seen a woman eat with as much enthusiasm as Shannon had at the rehearsal dinner the night before.

Her loose, short curls framed her round face and lent her an angelic look that probably gave many men the wrong impression. She wasn't sugar and spice—far from it. Inside that soft, appealing package lurked the hardened heart of a warrior.

Or did it?

He had been watching her now for two days. The cool, tough persona she offered him was not the one she shared with her family. Watching her interact with her brothers and her cousins, Thorsten saw what he believed was the real her: a woman of humor, of charm, of genuine softness toward those she loved. He saw it in the way she looked at them, laughed with them, teased them. When she was relaxed, her guard down, she could light up the room like a bonfire.

Why not enjoy his holiday? He hadn't expected a diversion like this, but why not see how far he could take it? Thorsten appreciated a challenge—it was why he climbed glaciers and kayaked open seas and backpacked alone in the Icelandic wilderness. If not for a little risk, how would he know what he was capable of? If not for the occasional gamble, who knew what prizes he might be missing?

Four days. Not much time, but if he played it right, that might be long enough.

. . .

THE PROBLEM WITH WEDDINGS, Shannon thought, was all the false expectations they created: that from then on life would be perfect, that love conquers all, that the formality of a wedding was all it took to bind two people together for life.

Her own wedding had been a simple affair of a judge, two witnesses, a bouquet of mixed buds from the florist strategically-located a block from the courthouse. She hadn't told anyone she was getting married until after the ceremony. That should have been a sign.

She rationalized it at the time as refusing to buy into all the pomp and expense of a traditional wedding. In truth, she was rushing ahead, afraid to look where she was going. She was twenty-three and felt certain she knew everything there was to know about men. Erik seemed as good a mate as any she'd met, and Shannon prided herself on her ability to make quick decisions. In retrospect, it was the one time she wished she had had a failure of nerve. The marriage lasted less than a year, but its lessons were permanently ingrained: Fast love is bad love. It can be fun, exciting, a physical thrill, but it doesn't last.

Love like Annie's? That lasted. Annie had fallen for Kjartan as quickly as Shannon had fallen for her husband, but the difference lay in the women themselves. Annie was sensible and cautious about her heart. She had held onto her virginity beyond the bounds of good sense, and seemed all the better for it. She didn't have that hard edge Shannon heard in her own voice sometimes when interviewing a prospective lover. Promises of love left Shannon cold. A threat of passion, however, always qualified as a winning answer.

But even that wasn't enough any more. She had spent too much energy the past few years speeding from one brief, intense affair to the next. She didn't have the heart for it anymore. The problem was, she didn't have the heart for more than that, either.

She hadn't always been so skeptical of romance, but having seen its darker side—in the infidelities of her parents and boyfriends, and the short unhappy course of her own marriage—she knew it was foolish to regard love with anything less than cynicism. She liked men, liked their company. Growing up with brothers like hers had imprinted her with a fundamental appreciation for men's finer qualities. But having a good time with a man did not mean she was ready to open herself up again to another hurt so deep and lasting as the one she had inflicted on herself almost a decade before. She was not marriage material—she knew it, and had set free any lover who was unwilling to believe her. Some people, like Annie, were made for it. Shannon clearly was not.

She wouldn't have minded a fling with Thorsten, but then what? Shake his hand at the airport and add another gold star to her calendar? Besides, she was much more interested in her long-term relationship with her brothers than with the flash of passion Thorsten might offer. She had come to Tucson to have a good time with her family and to watch her cousin marry the man she loved. She hadn't come to embroil herself in whatever passed for an Icelandic mating ritual.

No, she had made up her mind and would stick to her plan. Once she decided nothing was going to happen with a man, she always managed to extricate herself before the flirtation went too far. Just like a judge slamming down her gavel: *Case dismissed. Next case.*

Thorsten's hand rested easily in the small of her back. She hadn't seen him come toward her. Shannon felt a shock of heat moving from her spine down her legs.

"Let's be friendly," Thorsten urged her. "Come dance with me."

*Just say no.*

"All right." She let him take her hand and lead her onto the dance floor. When he drew her in, she went. She laid her cheek against his chest, let her body rest lightly against his. She could feel his heartbeat against her cheek. She shifted away, but he pulled her in even closer than before.

Thorsten folded her hand into his chest and held it there almost protectively. He shuffled slowly, barely moving, holding her in an embrace so light she felt free, yet so charged with controlled intensity she had no doubt where the moment might lead them if she let it.

Shannon lifted her face and dared to look into his eyes. Thorsten dipped his head towards hers until his lips hovered just a breath away from hers.

"What do you want?" she asked. Her voice sounded strange to her own ears—timid, unsure.

Thorsten lifted her hand and kissed the inside of her wrist. She felt her pulse beating against his lips. He folded her hand into his chest and regarded her with a directness she hadn't expected. She looked away, conscious of the heat rising from her core. *No good, Shan. Handle it.*

"If you're coming on this backpacking trip because you

think something's going to happen between us, forget it right now," she warned him.

"That's not why I'm coming."

"Good."

His lips curved into a soft smile. His eyes were as provocative as his embrace.

"I'm here to have a good time with my family," Shannon continued. "I'm not interested in a fling. If you think you can behave yourself, then you can come along. But if you think you're crawling into my sleeping bag—"

"I'm shocked you would think that."

"I'm serious, Thorsten. Nothing puts me in a worse mood than being played when I don't want to be. If that's really why you're coming, don't bother. Stay here with Annie and Kjartan."

The soft sighs of violin gave way to bass and drums and a steady rock beat. Thorsten released his hold on her, but leaned close so she could hear. He was suddenly serious—a side of him she hadn't seen yet.

She could feel his lips vibrating against her ear. "I would like nothing better than to take you to bed," he said, "but I'm not going to work for it this hard. I like women who like me. I don't have to beg anyone."

Shannon's breath quickened. Heat flushed her cheeks. "I just wanted to be clear—"

"You were." He stood tall again, his expression betraying nothing.

"Okay." She felt awkward, foolish, as if she had misread the cues. But hadn't he admitted it? He said he wanted to take her to bed—she hadn't misunderstood.

"Good night," he said. He turned to go.

She gripped his arm. "Wait—" The music pounded in her head. She pulled Thorsten toward her so he could hear. "So, we'll just go on this backpack, right? No problems."

"No problems," he agreed. "I already told you, sugarplum —I can wait longer than you can."

2

"**H**ey, lazy," Michael called to Shannon, "you coming out?"

"In a minute."

This was one of her favorite things: to sit in her tent, swaddled in sleeping bag, watching the sun creep down the canyon walls, sipping coffee to warm and wake her, the blue fleece hat preserving her body heat, her feet warm in their socks. The men were up, sitting in camp chairs they'd made out of their sleeping pads, drinking coffee and quietly savoring the dawn. Shannon watched them through the mesh tent door, in no rush to join them.

At times like this she couldn't imagine herself back in the office, wearing pantyhose and high heels, taking calls from clients and other attorneys, preparing motions and appellate briefs and opinion letters. The job paid for her pleasures—her beautiful old house in downtown Minneapolis, the traveling, the outdoor toys—but life as a lawyer was less fulfilling than she imagined. She could do the work—it suited her style and temperament—but being good at her job was not the same thing as loving it.

She experienced two rival reactions toward her work: energetic engagement and utter apathy. When she was on, she was on. She could manage a case load that would bury another lawyer. She spent months going from one trial to the next, barely stopping to catch her breath before girding for war once again and charging off. She won trials, she lost them, but there was always the next thing tugging at her skirts for attention, so the highs were never too high and the lows never rock-bottom.

And then came the inevitable crash, when her brain couldn't take in one more fact, her mouth couldn't muster one more argument. She crawled home after days like that and stared at her calendar, counting the days until her next vacation.

When the firm offered her junior partner status, Shannon saw her opportunity. Instead of accepting the standard raise that came with the position, she had negotiated for more vacation time than anyone in the firm. She would ask for even more the next time she came up for review. What good was working so hard if she couldn't play that hard as well?

Now she took eight weeks off during the year. She worked as hard as ever for a few months at a time, and lived for that moment when she could close her files and leave without any remorse for what she was missing. She rarely called into the office when she was away. She didn't have that need some other lawyers in her office had to micromanage every aspect of her practice. She was good enough now that clients forgave her these disappearances. Shannon trained her staff not to bother her on vacation. When she was at the office, she was there one hundred percent, working seven days a week, twelve-hour days. When she was away, it was as though she had never heard of the firm.

Her social life seemed to follow a similar pattern. She went months without looking at men, happy to concentrate on work or her house or catching up on her sleep. Then a flirtation might snag her attention, and if it occurred close enough to one of her vacations, she might pursue it. She often combined first dates with skiing or mountain biking or hiking. No point in pursuing a relationship with someone who couldn't do what she wanted in what little free time she found.

"Thorsten's making your oatmeal," Michael prodded.

"All right, all right, I'm coming."

Shannon zipped up the inner door to her tent, blocking her from the men's view. She slipped out of her long johns into hiking shorts and a short-sleeved top. She pulled off her hat and combed her fingers through her curls.

Then she stopped herself. *Who are you doing that for? You wouldn't care how you looked if you were here with just the boys.*

She snugged the hat back on and added a layer of fleece pants and coat over her hiking clothes. She unzipped the tent and went out as-is.

Thorsten seemed to have taken equal care with his appearance. He wore Will's sweatpants— too short for him by a couple of inches— and his own long-sleeved cotton T-shirt, threadbare and stained. Shannon had never seen him in glasses. They made him look almost academic—serious. The twig tangled in his wavy brown hair added to the aura of absent-minded professor.

Shannon's brothers grunted to her, but Thorsten greeted her with a smile as warm as the advancing sun. "Good morning."

She couldn't resist smiling back. Apparently he didn't understand the convention of speaking as little as possible until after breakfast.

Shannon freshened her coffee and settled into her camp chair to watch Thorsten assemble breakfast. He poured maple-flavored instant oatmeal into four bowls, then topped each with walnuts, dried fruit, and heaping spoonfuls of dried milk. He added just enough boiling water to turn the concoctions into rib-sticking glue.

Her eyes lingered on Thorsten's as he handed her a bowl. *Definitely cute,* she had to admit. And, to his credit, a better camp cook than any man she'd ever met.

While making their final plans for the trip, Thorsten had offered to prepare all their meals, since the others had already supplied the food. Shannon and her brothers readily accepted—cooking was the least of their outdoor skills. The night before they left, Michael took Thorsten to the grocery store to pick up a few "extras." Already they had relished the delicious effect of those extras.

After their first day spent trudging down dusty canyon trails and up rocky hillsides, sweating under a warm April sun, Shannon and her brothers had treated themselves to a dip in the stream near their campsite. Thorsten stayed in camp to unpack the cooking gear and prepare his first course. He retrieved them from streamside once the soup was simmering.

Appetizers: cream of mushroom soup and crackers topped with Gorgonzola cheese and dried apricots. Dinner was angel hair pasta and spaghetti sauce supplemented with fresh garlic, rehydrated sun-dried tomatoes, fresh basil, and slivers of Parmesan. For dessert, Thorsten broke off squares of expensive European chocolate and sank them into mugs of hot cocoa.

Michael moaned contentedly as he sipped the rich chocolate. "Okay, Thorsten, I don't normally say this to guys, but...I think I love you, man."

Thorsten deepened his voice. "Thank you, Michael."

"If you were a woman," Michael continued, "I would definitely marry you." He turned to his big sister. "Want to handle that for us, Shan? Then he can come camping with us all the time."

"You mean like when you wanted me to go out with the Ferrari salesman?"

"Totally different," Michael said. "I admit that was just for me—but this is for all of us."

Shannon glanced at Thorsten over the rim of her mug. He caught her eye and winked. She quickly looked away.

"I need a wash," Thorsten announced when they were finished with the soup. "Can I change in your tent?"

"Sure," Chris answered, "but didn't you bring Will's tent?"

"No, I decided not to. I never get to sleep under the stars at home—it's always raining or too cold. This might be my only chance." He ducked into Chris and Michael's tent and changed into bright orange swim trunks, then hiked to the stream in the last of the evening's light.

Shannon's brothers took advantage of his absence.

"Well, I'd say he's trying pretty hard," Michael observed.

"No kidding," Chris agreed.

"Trying what?" Shannon asked.

"To impress you."

"What? No, he's not."

"Oh, really?" Michael said. "Do you think he'd be cooking like this for just me and Chris?"

"I don't know, maybe. You did tell him you loved him."

"So what's wrong with him?" Chris asked her. "Why don't you like him?"

"Nothing's wrong with him," Shannon answered defensively. "Why are you bothering me?"

"Because I kind of like him for you," Chris answered.

"I'm afraid you're not qualified to pick my men."

Michael snorted. "Neither are you. I remember the last guy—what was his name?"

"Oh, yeah," Chris nodded, "Barry, wasn't it? Isn't he the one who wouldn't stop talking?"

"Morning till night," Michael confirmed. "'Then I won this case,'" he mocked. "'Then I won that one. Then I made a million dollars. Then I bought fifteen Rolexes—one to go with each of my cars. Then I—'"

"He wasn't like that," Shannon protested.

Michael brushed her off. "He talked in his sleep, too— man, does he ever shut up? That was the longest backpacking trip I've ever been on, and it was only three days.

Now that one you were right to lose. But Thorsten—come on, there's nothing wrong with him."

"Other than the fact that he lives thousands of miles away and I just met him and I don't like him—other than that, you're right, he's perfect. Since when do you get to pick my boyfriends?"

"Since you started bringing them around for us to check out," Michael answered.

"What? I didn't ask Thorsten to come—you guys did!"

"It was for your own good," said Chris.

Michael nodded. "Someone has to do it. You obviously don't know how to pick them yourself."

"You know what, Baby Michael? I'm really not enjoying this anymore. I think you boys have had your fun. Can we drop it now?"

"I'm just saying," Michael persisted, "if Thorsten wants to give you the old nudge, you should take him up on it."

"Michael..."

He ignored her warning tone. "Just don't do it around us, okay? Let's keep this a clean family vacation. But who knows? Maybe we've finally found a guy for you that we can all stand."

"Thanks," Shannon answered dryly. "As always, your kindness astounds me. But how about if you let me pick my own—"

A twig snapped. Shannon's head jerked up. Thorsten ambled into camp. *How long had he been standing there?*

Chris grinned at his little sister. "What were you saying, Shan?"

"Nothing." The fading light didn't do justice to her menacing glare.

Thorsten disappeared inside Chris and Michael's tent. "Can I go with you to hang the bear bag?" he called. "I'd like to see what you do."

"Sure," Chris answered, still smirking at his sister, "but don't you hang your food in Iceland?"

"No," came the answer from the tent. "Two reasons: no trees, and no bears."

"Really?" Chris asked.

"No bears in summer anyway, which is the only time we backpack there. Sometimes in winter polar bears come over on ice floes from Greenland, but they don't get to stay long."

"Polar bears?" Michael mouthed to Shannon. He nodded as though greatly impressed.

Shannon rolled her eyes.

"And really," Chris asked, "no trees?"

"A few here and there, but we have a joke: 'What do you do if you're lost in a forest in Iceland? Stand up.' The trees are all pretty small, and there aren't that many of them left. The Vikings used them all to make houses and forgot to replant some more."

"Vikings," Michael murmured to Shannon. "Very manly."

She tried to seem bored.

Thorsten emerged from the tent dressed once more in sweat pants and T-shirt.

"Okay, so let's go," Chris said. "Everyone checked their packs, their pockets?" He turned to Thorsten. "Make sure you take out anything that has a scent to it—candy bars, toothpaste, sunscreen—everything."

Thorsten tossed a few more items into the food bags, then Chris cinched them tight. "Want to come, Shan?"

"No, thank you, I've done it before. But why don't you go, too, Baby Michael?"

"Sure." He leaned over her chair and added in a whisper, "Bossy Cow."

Now she knew why they hadn't revealed her nickname to Thorsten when they had the chance at Annie's wedding. They didn't want to spoil the budding romance—the romance they had conspired to create.

*Sweet, in a way,* Shannon thought. She liked the idea of her brothers making a project of improving her life. But this was going too far, and in the wrong direction. She needed to discourage them.

"I'm going to bed," she proclaimed. "See you all in the morning."

"This early?" Michael asked.

"Yep. Got a book to read." She zipped into her tent and dressed for bed while Thorsten and her brothers hung the food. They returned to camp laughing at some shared joke.

Shannon snuggled into her sleeping bag, turned on her headlamp, and opened her paperback. Normally she would have sat up with her brothers for at least another hour, catching up on the details of their lives since the last time they had gotten together for a backpacking trip the previous summer. Shannon knew the highlights—Chris's latest successes as a jazz musician, Michael's daring escape from a woman who nearly coaxed him to the altar, their middle brother Will's excursion to Guatemala as a volunteer engineer on a housing project—

but she missed hearing about the nuances of their daily lives.

They considered their parents erratic and unreliable, but the siblings had always been each others' solid, faithful supporters. Shannon needed trips like these to reconnect with her brothers. Now that Annie was married and caught up in her new life in Iceland, Shannon needed her brothers' attention even more.

How many more of these backpacking trips would they have together? Michael was in his mid-twenties now, Will and Chris in their mid-thirties—how much longer would she be able to preserve her close family bond with them, when at any moment some woman might come along and snatch the boys away from her? She doubted that a wife would be as tolerant of these sibling trips as the brothers' girlfriends had learned to be. And what if her brothers had kids some day? What wife would allow her husband to sneak away from the squalling kids and come hang out with his sister? Shannon knew her time with them was short, and yet here she was hiding out.

She pretended to read, but the words never reached her brain. Finally she switched off her headlamp and lay in her tent listening. Chris and Michael quizzed Thorsten about his life in Iceland, particularly his outdoor adventures and experiences as a guide. Thorsten talked of cross-country skiing over glaciers, kayaking in open seas, backpacking in a place called "the Horn," where the weather was harsh, the terrain tricky, and the views spectacular.

"You should come some time," he told the brothers. "The

company does trips all summer. I'll send you a schedule when I get back."

"You should take Shan," Michael said. "She'll be up there in June. What do you think, Shan?"

She pretended to be asleep.

"I'll be happy to take her if she wants to go," said Thorsten. "But you guys should think about it, too."

"Yeah, maybe I will," Chris answered. " Probably not this year, but maybe next. Sounds pretty wild."

"You should take Shannon," Michael repeated.

*A dart gun,* Shannon thought. *My kingdom for a dart gun...*

"I'd love to," Thorsten answered. "But that's her choice."

*Thank you. At least someone recognizes that.*

Chris murmured something Shannon couldn't hear. Michael laughed and said, "That's right."

*What? What's right?* Shannon fought the urge to run out there and break up the happy crew.

Michael added something, but his voice was too low to make out. If they meant to torture her, Shannon thought, they were doing a superior job.

"We'll see," Thorsten told the brothers. "That might take a while."

3

Heavens, she was well-made.

Thorsten watched her through the lens of his camera. The shutter whirred without her noticing. Another candid photo on Shannon in her element, like a seal gliding beneath the waves.

The group set out together on their second morning, but soon they spread out along the trail, each choosing his or her own pace. Thorsten often lagged behind, camera in hand, waylaid by some natural feature that captured his attention. He dipped his camera lens in the palette of Arizona color: the rosy orange of sunrise against the canyon walls; distant pale green slopes dotted with dark green juniper; rocks along the trail tinted purple and peach, like a fading bruise; a downy white feather trapped in the spires of a cactus.

Shannon didn't seem to notice those times he pulled her into the frame: Throwing back her head to laugh at something one of her brothers said; running her fingers through her sweat-dampened bangs; bending to swab blood from her leg with her faded blue bandana. Thorsten rarely photographed people—he had always preferred the shapes and colors and textures of nature—but occasionally a woman came along whom he had to capture on film. In Shannon's case, he wanted some proof once he was back in Iceland, to remind him why she affected him this way.

He tried not to look at her too much. Looking led to a physical reaction beyond his control. He guessed her brothers wouldn't appreciate him drooling over their sister, so he kept his eyes to himself. They might be encouraging him in theory to pursue her, but tangible evidence of his attraction to her might prove more than they could handle. He sensed that Shannon's brothers, for all their teasing, were protective of their sister. Thorsten had to tread carefully to keep them all on friendly terms.

But heavens, she was an eyeful. He caught a glimpse of her briefly when he called them for supper the night before. Her black bikini highlighted her round hips, her full breasts, her soft touchable belly. She was ripe in the right places, muscular in others, compact and nicely-proportioned, like a yoga instructor he had dated once. Lying on a warm rock, arm thrown over her eyes, the muscles in her arms and legs a perfect complement to the curves of her torso—she had composed the photograph for him so perfectly, he wished he had brought his camera down to the stream.

"Just make sure you tell her you don't ever want to get married," Chris had advised him the night before. "She's allergic to men who might actually love her."

Michael had confirmed that strategy. "But if you do want to marry her some day," he had added in a whisper, "let us know. We'll talk her into it for you. She's not so bad, once you get to know her."

"We'll see," Thorsten told them. "That might take a while."

What he didn't say was that he, too, had an aversion to marriage. While he was happy his older brother had remarried, Thorsten remembered too clearly the bitter ending of Kjartan's first marriage. Thorsten had been twenty-six at the time and involved with a woman he felt certain was the right one. Her reaction to the divorce had shown him otherwise.

"Serves him right," Gudrún had said. "He never should have quit his job in Reykjavik."

"What does that have to do with it?"

"Marta thought she married an architect, not a horse farmer. How's he ever going to make something of himself now?"

"He hated his work," Thorsten reminded her. "He loves that farm. I say he made the right choice."

"It was stupid. He made much more money in Reykjavik."

Gudrún was growing less attractive by the minute.

"What if I decide to work in the shrimp factory all my life?" he asked her.

She brushed it off. "You wouldn't do that. You're too smart."

"But what if I decided that's what would make me happy?"

"Then I would have to change your mind." She patted his arm sweetly, but her smile was cold.

He couldn't leave it alone. "What if I told you my idea of a perfect life is to live right here in this apartment you think is so shabby, and keep working in the factory all winter so I can guide in the summers?"

"It's fine for now," she said stiffly, "but you weren't planning on doing that all your life?"

"I don't know if I am or not, but I'd still like to know your answer."

Gudrún smiled uncertainly. "You're joking, huh? You know you deserve better—*I* deserve better. You must see that."

He was beginning to. Soon afterward they parted ways.

Now, at 33, Thorsten's life was much as he had described it to Gudrún that night. His work was simple, his hobbies absorbing. His ambitions were small and he had met them all. Life was good. He enjoyed the company of women, but that one near-marriage experience had cured him of the need for greater commitment.

From the sound of it, Shannon shared his attitude. And that made her all the more attractive.


THIS WAS EXACTLY what her body was made for, Shannon thought—these long-distance trudges with a heavy pack. She had shorter legs than the men, but what she lost in stride she made up for with endurance. While she liked sports of speed, none of them brought her this peace of mind, this time for quiet contemplation while her feet resolutely carried her over the earth.

The group broke for lunch—crackers piled with slices of salami and the last of the Gorgonzola cheese, trail mix, dried fruit. Thorsten rested casually beside her, his back against the same tree, his leg occasionally leaning against hers. His touch felt natural, light—not charged with intensity the way it had been at the wedding. She could handle this, Shannon decided. Nothing wrong with a little friendliness.

But as the afternoon wore on Thorsten found other excuses for touching her: grasping her elbow when she tripped, brushing his arm against hers as he passed, reaching for her hand to help her down from a boulder.

"I don't need that," she said, but she took his hand anyway.

"I know you don't," but he continued to offer it nonetheless.

They set up camp in an old horse corral near a stream. Shannon changed into her bikini, then covered it with her hiking shorts and shirt.

"Coming?" Chris asked Thorsten.

"Yes, I think I will this time."

Shannon hurried down to the water while Thorsten changed. If she were quick about it, she could be done rinsing off the sweat by the time he arrived.

*Why do you care? Treat him like one of the boys.*

But she did care, and the knowledge disturbed her.

Shannon tested the water—icy spring snowmelt from the mountain above. She waded in slowly, panting as the frigid water climbed up her legs, past her thighs, finally to her waist.

"Cold?" Chris asked.

"No!" She pressed her chattering teeth together. "It's warm! Come on in!"

She saw the flash of Thorsten's orange swim trunks as he came up the trail. Wasting no time, Shannon dove under the water to rinse the rest of her body. She popped up gasping from the cold. Then she hurried out of the pool, pulled on her shirt, and began drying her legs with a small pack towel.

"How's the water?" Thorsten asked.

"Freezing," Chris answered. He still stood ankle-deep waiting for the courage to wade further.

Thorsten charged in without hesitation. "Ah, this is nice. Wait until you feel the rivers near the Arctic Circle—you'll think this was like bath water."

"We were talking about that last night," Michael told Shannon. He obviously believed she had been asleep instead of eavesdropping. "Thorsten said you can go on one of his trips when you're over visiting Annie."

She avoided looking at Thorsten. "I don't know—I'm going to be pretty busy with Annie."

"Did she talk to you about kayaking?" Thorsten asked.

That got her attention. "No."

"Annie told me she'd like to try sea kayaking. She said you might do it with her, since Kjartan's too busy to leave the farm in summer. I'm leading a group the first weekend you're over there. The place isn't far from where they live."

*Tempting.* Shannon had canoed in the Boundary Waters

and done some river kayaking, but had never operated a small craft on the open seas. "I don't know—maybe."

"You should go backpacking while you're over there, too," Michael said. "Don't you have a trip she could go on, Thorsten?"

"Maybe," he answered, "I'll have to check."

"I'm going there to see Annie," Shannon reminded all of them.

"So go a little longer," Michael pressed, "and spend a few days with Thorsten. When else are you going to get a chance to backpack in Iceland?"

Shannon shrugged noncommitedly. The conversation was rapidly getting out of hand. Soon she'd be agreeing to all sorts of foolish schemes.

*Play it out*, her analytical brain said—*what do you think can happen?*

*Worst case? Come on—you know where it would lead. A fling with a charming, handsome man. A hot, steamy affair. Nights of passion and pleasure.*

*And then?*

*The usual. Over too soon. Back to work.*

*So?*

*So we're not doing that anymore. Too little return for the investment. There's no point in it. Get a dog.*

"No, thanks," Shannon told them. "Think I'll hang out with Annie and Kjartan."

Thorsten didn't surrender easily. "But if she wants to come kayaking, you'll come too?"

The familiar dance of negotiation. "Maybe," Shannon answered. "We'll see."

Thorsten dove under water and stayed there an inhumane amount of time. When he emerged his skin look scalded by the cold.

He splashed back to the bank and reached a dripping hand toward Shannon. "Is that a deal?"

"That I'll think about it? Sure, I guess so." *What's the harm in that?* She shook his icy palm.

"Good," Thorsten said. "Anyone ready to eat?"

Hummus on pita bread. Jambalaya—spicy rice with smoked sausage, sun-dried tomatoes, dried soup greens. Hot cocoa with raspberry-filled chocolate squares melting in the bottom of the mugs.

"How much food are you packing?" Chris asked. "No wonder you couldn't bring Will's tent—no room."

"Three nights of food is easy," Thorsten answered. "It's much heavier if I'm going out more than a week."

"You cook like this all the time?" Michael asked, exchanging a look with Chris.

"Yes, if I have clients. Not so much if I'm alone."

"I'm serious, Thorsten," Michael said, "you could be the best camp cook I've ever met. You're welcome any time you want to come out with us again."

"Thanks." Thorsten glanced up at Shannon, his expression unreadable. Was he looking for her approval?

Shannon saw no need to withhold it—he really was a marvel. "It's fantastic," she agreed. "Thanks for doing all this."

"No problem."

Over the past two days Shannon had noticed the change. He wasn't the man who had breathed warmly against her neck while they danced, who had whispered seductively or flirted with her at every turn. He was easy, relaxed—which meant she could relax, too. She preferred him this way, when he wasn't trying so hard.

Still, she couldn't relax entirely. Whether or not he was trying anymore, the fact remained that she felt his presence like an electrical field, making her skin warm and her fingers tingle. Every time he brushed against her she felt herself move into the touch. Yes, she admitted to herself as she had hiked along, she would have liked to start something if he were anyone else. If Thorsten lived anywhere near Minneapolis, she might put some effort into discovering what fire burned beneath that cool, cocky exterior. She might, despite her better judgment, let her body take what it wanted before her head had time to sort out the details.

But her head was still firmly in charge. Thorsten could be nothing more than a one-night stand—a two-night at most—and she wasn't looking for another one of those. The thrill of the chase always gave way to the reality of the capture. Thorsten hardly seemed the type to disprove her cynicism about romance. He was a charmer, no question about it. Unfortunately, experience had proven that the more charming the man, the more bitter the inevitable end. There was a price to pay for the highs of romance, and Shannon was tired of losing her shirt.

Thorsten handed her a steaming mug of cocoa. She sipped slowly, savoring the comfort of smooth rich chocolate melting on her tongue. What a luxury. What a gem Thorsten had turned out to be.

She couldn't help it. She lifted her eyes to his and didn't look away.

His eyes were a soft Nordic blue. He gazed at her with a familiarity that made her feel exposed, but also understood. He was close enough that she could have reached out and laid her hand on his cheek, drawn him closer, tasted the chocolate from his own lips. She knew with certainty that she would have kissed him just then, if they had only been alone.

The thought brought heat to her cheeks. But still she didn't look away. His eyes warmed, his mouth curved into the hint of a smile.

But they weren't alone. Her brothers were watching. Shannon sat up straight and concentrated on her cocoa. She glanced guiltily at Michael, and immediately regretted it.

"What?" she challenged him.

"Nothing," her little brother smirked. "How's that hot chocolate?"


WITH EACH NEW delicacy he placed before her, he saw her melt a little more. By the time she tasted the chocolate, a dazed smile of satisfaction had crept onto Shannon's lips. In that moment Thorsten knew the extra weight of all that food in his pack was worth it.

Heavens, she was beautiful.

He had thought she was attractive before, when she wore city clothes and a hint of makeup, but out here she was stunning. Dressed in shorts and hiking boots that showed off her smooth, muscular legs, her cheeks rosy from sun and exertion, her damp hair clinging to her temples and the base of her neck—he couldn't look at her without wanting to touch her. He imagined cradling the back of her head in his hand, lowering his mouth to hers, tasting her and feeling her respond. That was what he wanted most—to feel her give in to his touch, instead of always joking him away. Was she that tough? Was she that immune to him?

He thought he had felt a change as the day wore on and he found more excuses to touch her. She didn't tense up the way she used to. She seemed to move into his touch. Maybe this campaign was working. Maybe she could be seduced after all.

He had boasted to her he could wait longer than she could, but now he knew it wasn't true. If she would give in just a little—show him she was willing to let go—he would gladly guide her the rest of the way.

He meant what he said at the wedding—he wouldn't beg. He wanted a woman to want him. And Shannon did—he was almost sure of it.

If only she would admit it.


SHE STAYED up with them this time. The thought of crawling into her tent alone and lying awake listening to them talk made her feel empty and cold. This was her vacation, her few precious days to be with her brothers—she wouldn't spend the time hiding from Thorsten.

Besides, it might be nice to stay up with him, too.

They used the existing fire ring at the campsite and built a small fire of their own.

"I don't get to do this very often," Thorsten told them as he warmed his hands over the flames. "The only wood where we backpack is driftwood from the ocean, and it's usually too wet for a fire."

"What do you do to keep warm?" Shannon asked.

Thorsten shot her a suggestive look. "We have ways. You should come find out."

Chris must have noticed the sultry tone of Thorsten's voice, because he switched topics immediately. "How's that camera you use? I've been wanting one like that."

Thorsten didn't miss a beat. "You can try mine tomorrow. See if you like it."

Shannon observed with amusement Chris's diversionary tactic. Her brothers might think they wanted to find her a boyfriend, but the reality of their sister actually having sex with a man had always been too much for them. The few times she had dared bring a lover on one of their family trips, she had lectured him ahead of time on a strict code of behavior: no kissing, no petting, no lewd remarks. Out there you're just another brother—understand?

Michael asked, "Do you just take landscapes?"

"Most of the time." Thorsten poked at the fire with a stick. "I look for unusual colors or shapes. There's a lot of nice color out here."

The remark surprised her. Shannon had always found this area in the wilderness outside of Tucson to be fairly colorless—mostly brown and dusty green. The beauty of the place was in the challenge it brought to her physically. The trails were rugged and steep. The water sources were spaced far apart, so their daily mileage had to be substantial if they wanted to camp by a stream every night. She liked the ache in her thighs at the end of the day, that soreness in her shoulders from ferrying a heavy pack. This exertion was what she craved, to allow her mind to relax.

Shannon stirred the coals and added another log. "Too bad we don't have marshmallows. You didn't bring any did you, Thorsten?"

"No, sorry."

"Ah, the one time you fail us." Against her better judgment, she smiled softly.

Thorsten leaned forward. The fire illuminated his eyes and revealed a yearning that matched her own. "I wasn't sure what you might want."

*What I want...*

What she wanted was to move her chair closer to his, lean against him and share the warmth of the flames. What she wanted was to feel the comfort of his thigh against hers and his strong arm across her shoulders.

What she wanted was to forget the arguments against it, and to let herself fall into whatever trouble Thorsten was offering.

She wanted to be alone with him right now. Wanted to say what she was thinking—wanted to show him.

Thorsten stood and stretched. "I think I'll say goodnight."

"Yeah," Shannon agreed, even though she wasn't the slightest bit tired. "Me, too. Good night, boys."

"'Night, Shan."

She unzipped her tent.

*What just happened? Why the retreat?*

She changed into long underwear tops and bottoms and

a pair of cotton socks. She pulled on the blue fleece hat and burrowed into her sleeping bag. It would be so much warmer if he were where he belonged, beside her instead of out there...

*Stop it. Go to sleep. Have some sense for once.*

An hour passed, then two. Chris and Michael snored inside their tent. Thorsten breathed softly. Was he lying awake just like she was? Was he thinking of her? So what if he was?

*It would be so easy,* she thought. *Go out there. Motion for him to follow. Take him down to the water...*

*Stop it. Go to sleep.*

Shannon sighed and pulled her bag tightly over her head. Maybe if she couldn't hear him it would be easier to ignore how close he was, how accessible he was.

Eventually she slept, but not long enough. She awoke sleep-deprived and irritable. Even Michael's cheerful call was like the buzz of a dentist's drill.

"Coffee, sunshine?"

She groaned and turned her back to the tent door. Michael unzipped it anyway and nudged her with the mug.

"Come on. We have a lot of miles to do today. Time to get up."

Grudgingly she rolled toward him and accepted the brew. Over Michael's shoulder she could see Thorsten. Hair askew, face scruffy with stubble, eyes bearing bags she imagined rivaled hers.

*Good. At least that's something.*

But then he smiled at her, just like he did the morning before.

*Damn. Cut it out. Do you have to be so cute?*

She zipped away the sight and sat up to drink her coffee.

*Just two more days. Hang on. It's not so hard.*

Thorsten's voice at the door of her tent: "I forgot something."

She pulled down the zipper just enough to admit his eyes. "Yes?"

He coaxed the zipper further and reached in. He dropped two chocolate-covered espresso beans in her mug. "You look like you need it. I know I do."

He zipped up the tent before she could answer.

The tingling she felt wasn't from the cold.

4

It was almost laughable, all the excuses he found to touch her. Adjusting a strap on her pack that he said was loose. Offering his hand to help her up onto rocks or down from them. Holding back a branch that was guaranteed to snap her in the face, and waiting while she scraped past him. He wasn't lascivious about it, wasn't gawking at her or making any suggestive remarks. He simply put himself in her way from morning until late afternoon and seemed to dare her keep her distance.

The creek near their campsite that night was too shallow for a full dip. Shannon splashed water onto her arms and chest to wash away the top layer of sweat. She ran wet fingers through her hair.

Thorsten left them creekside—to begin cooking dinner, Shannon assumed.

When she and her brothers returned to camp, Thorsten offered a surprise. He dipped his fingers in the pot sitting on top of the backpacking stove. "Warm water," he said. "I thought you might like a shampoo."

Shannon glanced nervously at her brothers. They looked back with just the expressions she dreaded.

"Go ahead," Michael told her.

"You could use it," Chris said.

The brothers were having way too much fun.

"Fine," she answered defiantly. "I think I will."

Thorsten set the pot on a rock and placed their second pot on the stove.

Shannon knew the sensible thing would have been to remove her shirt and wear just her bikini top, but that was more exposure than she wanted. She tucked her pack towel into the collar of her shirt and accepted the clean mug Thorsten offered.

"Would you like me to do it?" he asked.

"No." Shannon glowered at her brothers. They pretended to concentrate on gathering kindling for a fire.

Shannon dipped the mug into the pot, leaned forward, and poured deliciously-warm water over her head. After her dip in the freezing creek, this was heavenly. She squirted dish soap into her palm and began working it into her scalp.

*Why is he still standing there?*

She reached blindly for the mug.

"Here. Let me." Thorsten poured a steady stream of water over her head. He worked his fingers into her scalp, tugging at the curls, coaxing the suds free.

It was almost too much to bear. She thought about pushing his hand away—or maybe covering it with her own as a promise of things to come. Shannon could barely breathe, for fear a moan might escape. She turned her head slightly and caught the mischievous glint in Thorsten's eyes.

*You know exactly what you're doing to me, don't you?*

"Wait," he said.

He returned with the second pot and poured it in one great cascade. There it was—the moan she had been holding back. Thorsten threaded his fingers through her curls one more time. His hands lingered there far too long. "There. I think I got it all."

Shannon squeezed the ends of her hair and stood up. She met Thorsten's gaze and took in his satisfied smile. Clearly he knew he had won this round.

Her brothers knew it, too. They stared at her with unabashed amusement.

Shannon tried to sound nonchalant. "Baby Michael, you're next."

"No, thanks. I like the way I stink."

"Chris?" she tried.

"Nah, I'm hungry. I'd rather Thorsten made soup in one of those pots."

She had run out of clever things to say. Mumbling that she had to change clothes, Shannon retreated to her tent.

*May we have a recess, your Honor? Counsel needs to gather her wits.*

Dinner was cream of asparagus soup, triangles of thin black bread, thick egg noodles with soy sauce, melted peanut butter, and crushed cashews. Airline-sized bottles of red wine. The last of the chocolate.

Shannon licked her spoon appreciatively. She tried to appear casual. "Really great, Thorsten. Thanks."

"No problem. I'm happy you like it, Shannon."

His gaze was so direct—so open and honest and so unreservedly intimate—she had to look away. How could he know her like this? He couldn't. It was just an act—some slick technique he had honed over years to coax women out of their parkas. He pretended to see right through her defenses, but it was only a game. Shannon had to admit he was good—maybe the best she'd seen so far—but that only meant she had the chance to improve her own game. If she could resist a pro like Thorsten, she could resist all those amateurs out there.

But it still didn't hurt to imagine...

After dinner Chris and Michael left to hang the bear bag. Thorsten stayed behind. Shannon sat in her camp chair, leaning against a rock, her foot no more than an inch from his.

She imagined this: closing the distance between them, stealing these few moments to take what she wanted. Touching him, kissing him, straddling him in the dirt, pinning his arms with her knees, warning him not to tell her brothers or else...

He was too quiet. Shannon realized her breathing had quickened. She looked up, locked eyes with Thorsten in the waning light. He knew. He knew everything she had been thinking. She saw it in his subtle smile and the dark intensity of his gaze. His leg brushed against hers. A charge jolted through her nerves.

"Bad idea," she murmured, surprised to hear herself say the words aloud.

He didn't answer. His gaze never wavered. His leg settled

against hers.

*Where are they? Just when I need chaperones...*

"Really bad idea," she repeated. Was she trying to convince him, or herself?

Thorsten's voice was husky and low. "I don't think so."

It took more willpower than she thought she had to stand and pick up her chair. "Thanks for dinner. Good night." She turned toward her tent and didn't look back. Once inside the safety of those fabric walls she could breathe again. But he was still too close—just a few feet away—and she could feel the heat rising from her core to meet that magnetic pull.

She knew now that she was as responsible as he was for all those little touches throughout the day. She put herself in his way. She lingered when she should have moved on. She had felt the draw of his physical presence and she responded, pretending to herself that she wasn't. But now she knew the truth.

She wanted him—*now*. For however many nights he could give her. She wanted to slip out of her tent, go to him, whisper in his ear, "Come with me." Take him down the trail to the smooth rock ledge above the creek, strip him bare, feel his hands on her breasts, his mouth on her skin, tease him and test him and when she couldn't wait any longer, draw him deep inside her and do it all quietly so no one would hear.

Shannon dove deeper into her sleeping bag and pulled it over her head.

*Stop it! Now.* She squeezed her eyes shut and tried to think of anything but the man sitting just outside her tent talking with her brothers now, waiting, it seemed, for her to make the first move.

Morning would come soon enough, wouldn't it? Sleep would come eventually, right? She lay entombed in self-discipline, wishing for all the world she could be reckless again just this once.

*Come on...give in...*

The thought was as seductive as if Thorsten had whispered it himself.

Just one more day, and she would be free of him.

One more day of pretending that was what she wanted.


It must have been the wine. Shannon awoke in the middle of the night with a need she could not suppress.

She slipped on her boots, tied them loosely, and as silently as possible unzipped the tent. Moonlight beamed through the door. She glanced toward Thorsten, who lay on his side with his back to her. She tiptoed down the trail away from camp. When she was out of sight and earshot she relieved the pressure on her bladder, then headed back up the trail.

Thorsten stood waiting for her.

Shannon froze. Moonlight lit Thorsten's face. He raised his finger to his lips, but she already knew they would have to be quiet.

He stepped toward her. She held her ground. Slowly he raised his hands to the sides of her face. Shannon lifted her mouth to his. She took from him the kiss she had needed since he drew her in on the dance floor.

She didn't want to notice she had given in. She didn't want to admit that this was her need, her mouth hungry for his, her body pressing against his, searching for what he might give her if she pushed him far enough. He slipped his hand beneath her top and stroked his fingers across her belly. Shannon suppressed the moan in her throat.

They had to be quiet—that thought kept running through her mind. Her brothers mustn't hear. She tried not to breathe too hard, let go too much. She was careful how she touched Thorsten so that he could control himself as well.

Her fingers brushed lightly across his groin. She was pleased with the effect. He kissed her more deeply, explored her bare belly and back, always careful to stop just shy of her breasts.

*Don't stop there,* she wanted to tell him. *Go on—keep going.*

They stood on the path where anyone might find them. Shannon pushed the thought away. She didn't want to stop. She didn't want to think.

His breath was hot against her ear. "Tell me what you want."

*You have to ask?* She nipped hungrily at his neck.

"Tell me," he insisted.

Shannon wrapped one leg around his, challenging both their balance. She needed to be closer, much closer. "Everything," she answered breathlessly.

And that's when she realized what he was doing.

He was playing with her. His satisfied smile confirmed it.

Shannon pushed away. "No," she whispered. Her heart raced, her nerves pulsed. Her body yearned for his. It would be so easy to shift toward him again, pull him off the trail to somewhere secluded, make love to him in the moonlight.

But he wanted it to be her decision. What had he said? "I can wait longer than you can." That was the game, wasn't it? Wasn't that why he kept asking her to tell him what she wanted?

Thorsten's eyes narrowed. The lust she read there was unmistakable. "No?"

Shannon grew stronger with every moment. Hard nipples showed through the thin fabric of her shirt, announcing her body's position on the matter, but her head was suddenly clear again.

Shannon turned and strode back up the trail. Thorsten caught her arm. She waited, not knowing what she wanted him to say or do next. Her lips throbbed for his kiss. Her arms longed to draw him to her, to erase any distance between them. For him she might have abandoned her modesty in the presence of her brothers, and risked them overhearing her sighs. It all might begin with a kiss...

But he didn't kiss her. Instead, he whispered, "Come visit me in Iceland."

It was the last thing she expected to hear. "What?"

"I want to take you backpacking."

Confusion mixed with hunger and unsteady resolve. "I don't know," she whispered, her mind muddled by the insistent demands of her body. *Kiss me. Shut up and kiss me.*

"You'd like it there."

"I don't know," she repeated. She pulled away, irritated now. Was the whole thing so easy for him? How could he come to her with such passion, then disengage so quickly?

Why was he talking about Iceland at a time like this? Was it all just a game to see how far he could make her go?

Shannon stalked up the trail alone. She slipped back into her tent and quietly zipped the door. She removed her boots and wrestled back into her sleeping bag. Her ears buzzed with adrenaline. Where was he now? Did he expect her to come racing back to him?

In time he returned to camp. She listened to his sleeping bag scuffle against the dirt. She lay awake, expecting to see him at any moment outside her tent, inviting her to come out and play. She lay awake listening with annoyance to his steady breath, wishing she had fallen asleep before he did. He was obviously accustomed to seduction. She thought she was, too, but not this time. Thorsten definitely had the upper hand, and that was completely unacceptable. Tomorrow she would do better. Tomorrow he could come to her naked with rehydrated roses and a miniature bottle of champagne, and she wouldn't flinch.

But boy, he could kiss. After an experience like that, a woman stayed kissed. Shannon awoke with lips still slightly swollen, with a body still aching for his hands to find her, for his hips to press against hers, for his need to be as great as hers.

And with a mind more resolved than ever not to let him near her.

ANNIE MET them at the trailhead the following afternoon. "How was it?"

"Great," Shannon answered with the enthusiasm of a

sullen child. She loaded her pack into the back of Annie's jeep and claimed the front seat for herself. The men squeezed together in back.

While the men chattered to Annie about the trip, Shannon stared out the window at the passing desert landscape. The day had been awful—awkward, strange, and in an odd way, too short. She might have figured out more if she'd had more time. As it was, her mind still reeled with questions about what had happened the night before, and where she and Thorsten stood.

Back at Annie's house, Shannon indulged in a long, hot shower. Then Annie put her to work.

True to form, Annie had used her vacation from teaching to squeeze in both a wedding and a move. She and her brothers had spent their time since the wedding sorting through the family house, dividing the last of their late mother's possessions. While the siblings sifted through photo albums and family treasures, Kjartan loaded boxes of dishware and books for shipment to Iceland, and boxed whatever items Annie's brothers wanted for themselves. They had worked efficiently—the house was nearly packed. Annie's brothers had left that morning.

"Some honeymoon," Shannon remarked as she loaded clothes into a box for charity.

"We'll honeymoon when we get back," Annie answered. "I'm not worried about it." She scrutinized her cousin. "Why are you being such a grump?"

Shannon shrugged. "I don't know. No reason."

"Yeah, why would you tell me?" Annie said. "I barely know you."

Shannon sighed and cracked a smile. "Sorry. I don't mean to be such a pill."

"So why don't you tell me?"

Shannon stood and closed the bedroom door. She sat back down on the carpet and leaned against the bed. "Why do I keep doing this?"

"Doing what?"

"Falling for someone who's so obviously wrong for me."

"What happened?"

"Nothing. A little kissing. But I wanted it to be a lot more—that's the problem."

"Why is that a problem?" Annie asked.

"Because he leaves tomorrow. Not much point in pursuing anything, even if I wanted to."

"But you do want to," Annie pointed out.

"You see why it's a problem."

"So let me get this straight: You like him. He, presumably, likes you—"

"I wouldn't count on that. He's a lot more devious than we give him credit for."

"Come on, Shan. You're not serious. If he kissed you he must like you."

Shannon groaned and covered her face with her hands. "Uchh, this sounds so junior high. If anyone saw me acting like this no client would ever hire me again." She looked up. "All right, yes—I think he likes me."

"And you'll be seeing him again in June. So why can't you wait and see what happens then?"

Shannon smiled wryly. "I'm not a wait-and-see kind of girl. I like to know where I stand."

"So ask him."

"Right."

"Okay," Annie said, "then forget about him."

Shannon nodded. She could still taste his kiss. The way his hands stroked her belly, never venturing high enough...

"Yeah. That's what I'll do. I'll forget him."

Annie added the last of her clothes to the box and taped it closed. "So I guess I shouldn't tell you what he said."

"What, did he put a note in your locker?"

"No, but he did say you agreed to go kayaking with him if I still wanted to go. I told him I did. We're supposed to meet him a few days after you arrive."

Shannon studied her cousin's face. "Don't act so innocent."

Annie laughed. "What? I am innocent. I want to try sea kayaking with my favorite cousin, and my new brother-in-law said he'd take us. What's wrong with that?"

"You're trying to get me to move to Iceland, aren't you? You think you can hook up the two of us and I'll move there just like you."

"It would be fun. I'd be your best friend."

"Did you talk to my brothers? Are you all in this together?"

"See?" Annie said. "They think it's a good idea, too."

Shannon groaned. "It's not going to work. I don't know how I got my nickname—it's the rest of you who are bossy."

"I'm not trying to boss you," said Annie. "I just think you look cute together."

"Puppies are cute. I'll get you one."

"You like him, though—admit it."

Shannon sighed. "Yes, I like him—all right? Too much, if you must know."

"Good. That's what I thought."

Shannon squinted suspiciously. "What are cooking up in that devious mind of yours?"

"Who, me? Let me just remind you of those three immortal words you wrote to me last summer when I was trying to decide what to do about Kjartan. Do you remember?"

"No, but I'm sure you do."

"'Go for it.'"

"Not the same thing."

"It could be."

"No. Different men, different women."

Annie smiled knowingly. "We'll see."

"You sound like Baby Michael."

"You always said you wanted someone your brothers would like," Annie reminded her.

"Yeah, but this one's not feasible. Trust me—I have a hard enough time dating men in my own city."

"We'll see."

"Annie—" The knock on the door interrupted any further lecture.

Thorsten stuck his head in. "Pizza is here."

"Thanks," Annie answered. "We'll be right out." She waited for him to shut the door again. "Aww-fully cute."

Shannon pointed to herself. "Aww-fully uninterested."

"That's such a lie."

"Prove it."

## 5

---

Pizza and a healthy dose of beer. Thorsten leaned back in his chair and patted his stomach. "Ahhh. Good, American food." He glanced toward Shannon. She still wouldn't look at him.

She sat on the couch next to Annie, stuffing pizza in her mouth, talking and laughing as though Annie were the only person in the room.

She had avoided him in camp, on the trail, and now back in civilization. Two steps forward, three steps back...

Chris reached for another slice. "When do you leave?"

Thorsten tore his eyes away from her. "Tomorrow at noon."

"Hmm, noon...that's a problem." Chris looked over his shoulder. "Shan, what're you doing tomorrow?"

"Helping Annie."

Chris turned back to Thorsten and winked. "You're going to have to take Thorsten to the airport."

She glared at her brother with unmistakable irritation. "Why? Can't you?"

"Nope. Annie ordered the moving truck. We'll be loading furniture all day."

Shannon turned to her cousin and whispered something. Thorsten didn't need to read lips to know what she asked.

Annie shook her head, bless her. A few words more, and he could see Shannon had been defeated.

"Fine," she answered. "I'll take you." Finally, she looked at him.

He met her eyes and smiled. "Thank you. That would be nice."

"Sure," she mumbled, and went back to devouring her pizza. He liked a woman who wasn't afraid to eat.

Later in the evening Annie made up the couch for him. Chris and Michael slept in Annie's brothers' old bedroom, Shannon slept in Annie's. Kjartan and Annie stayed in the master bedroom.

"This couch isn't great," Annie apologized to Thorsten. "There are a few loose springs. I hope it won't be too bad."

"I want to kiss your cousin."

Annie's eyes widened. "You're not supposed to tell me that."

"Why not?"

"This is America. We don't tell each other things like that."

"I was hoping you would help me."

"How? By holding her down?"

"No, by sneaking me into her room tonight."

"I would never do something like that."

"I didn't think so," he said. "So how about this? Tell me how to get her out of the house."

Annie looked at her watch. "It's pretty late."

"But you know how to do it."

"Well…"

Thorsten smiled at his sister-in-law. "Come on. I let you marry my brother."

Annie laughed. "Oh, you did? Funny, I don't remember you being involved in that."

"You just don't know—he does everything I say. I told him, 'That Annie, she's a prize—'"

Annie held up her hand. "Spare me the charm. You'll need all of it for Shannon."

But the charm seemed to work. Annie told him what he needed to know.

"She's my favorite cousin," Annie warned him.

"Mine, too."

"You mess this up, and I'm not inviting you for Christmas."

"I won't mess this up. I like her. That's why I want to kiss her."

"Don't tell me that."

"Why? My brother tells me that about you all the time."


SHANNON SAT in bed with the light on and a book open on her lap. She couldn't read a word.

*Why are you acting like this? What do you hope to accomplish?*

*Peace of mind, preserving my dignity—all the usual stuff.*

*Go out there and grab him.*

*Shut up and read your book.*

She heard the scrape of paper as it slid under her door.

It was so foolish, she couldn't resist smiling.

She padded to the door and retrieved the note.

COME GET ICE CREAM WITH ME.

She crushed her toes into the carpet and tried to make up her mind.

She opened the door.

"Nice pajamas," Thorsten said.

Shannon glanced down at her pajamas—white satin decorated with clusters of cherries. "Thanks."

"Will you come out with me?"

"No."

Thorsten stepped closer. He smelled of soap and shampoo—not at all like the night before. "Please?"

Shannon shook her head. Her pulse sped through her veins. She couldn't think clearly with him so near.

Thorsten stepped even closer and rested his hand on her hip. Shannon's breath quickened. Thorsten leaned forward and brushed his lips softly against her temple.

*Where is your willpower?*

"Get out," she murmured. "I have to change."

"Let me help." His smile was sexy beyond belief.

She flattened her palms against his chest and gently pushed him through the door. "Give me a minute. Are you buying?"

"Will they take credit cards?"

She rolled her eyes. "Freeloader. I'll buy." She closed the door and rested her forehead against it.

*Is this smart?*

*Definitely not. Hurry. Get dressed.*

Something about walking through her cousins' old neighborhood past dark, on the way to their favorite old ice cream parlor, made Shannon sentimental for more innocent times. Maybe she was making all of this too hard. Maybe she had forgotten how to live an uncomplicated life.

Shannon unfolded her arms from their secure position across her chest. She reached for Thorsten's hand.

"Don't say anything, all right?" she told him.

"I wasn't."

They sat at a pink metal table that had curlicue legs and ate with pink plastic spoons. Thorsten kept hold of her hand. The gesture warmed her in a way their passion the night before couldn't. This was the kind of date she never had. It reached her heart through a secret passage she didn't know existed.

So many times she could have pulled away. She forced herself to relax. They held hands on the walk home and spoke very little. Thorsten seemed to understand as well as she did how easily the spell could be broken.

He walked her to her bedroom door. At the threshold he kissed her chastely. "Good night."

"Good night," she whispered. She closed the door behind her and sank onto the bed. Her body tingled from one end to the other, inside out. She draped an arm over her eyes and waited for the dizziness to pass.

*What on earth was that? What is this guy up to?*

*What are you up to?* her conscience answered. *You were there, too.*

Shannon stripped off her clothes and slipped back into

her cherry pajamas. She pulled the covers to her chin in a classic display of modesty.

How was she supposed to sleep now? What kind of strange, Icelandic courtship was this?

If she slept, she didn't notice. Dawn found her drowsy but awake.

A light knock on the door.

"Yeah?"

Thorsten leaned in and set a cup of coffee on the carpet. He closed the door without a word.

Shannon smiled. *Whatever this is, I'd like to get used to it.*

Thorsten cooked for the family one last time. Eggs scrambled with cheese, mushrooms, and onions. Toast with Swiss cheese and jam. Multiple pots of Viking-strength coffee.

Her brothers seemed sad to see him go. They shook hands warmly and exchanged promises to do a trip together the following year. Annie hugged him and said she would see him at Christmas. Kjartan hugged his brother, too. Different though they were, Shannon could see a genuine affection between them.

There wasn't much to say. They drove in silence most of the way. As they neared the airport Shannon thought she should at least ask him about his itinerary.

"I fly to Minneapolis today, then to Reykjavik tomorrow night."

"Tomorrow night? When Annie flew from here last summer she did it all in one day."

"I couldn't get a good flight to Minneapolis tomorrow. It's cheaper to go today and stay in a hotel."

"A hotel, huh? So what are you going to do at a hotel all day tomorrow?"

"I don't know—swim, work on my awesome tan—"

"You're whiter than I am," Shannon pointed out.

"That's why I have to work on it."

When they reached the airport she left him at the ticketing area and parked the car. By the time she found him again she had made up her mind.

"Here." She handed him a key.

"What's this?"

"It's my house. I'm about twenty minutes from the Minneapolis airport." She asked the ticket agent for a scrap of paper, and drew Thorsten a map. She pointed the pen at him. "No parties, no fires, understand?"

"I promise."

Shannon folded the slip of paper and laid it in his palm. She took a deep breath. "Okay. I'm trusting you. Leave the key under the flower pot in back. And don't go through my underwear drawer."

"I'm going to wear every one of them."

"Fine. Take pictures." She turned him bodily and marched him toward the security checkpoint. "Okay, Thorsten, this is it."

"No, it's not. Come here." He took her hand and drew her all the way outside the terminal.

"You're going to be late."

"There's always time for this." He pulled her away from the crowds and wrapped her in his arms and kissed her as she wished he had the night before, when they were alone and had more time. It was the kiss of high school sweethearts just discovering each other, of lovers separated too long, of a man sure of his place in the heart of the woman he kissed.

*I've been drugged.* Shannon's mind swirled with sensual confusion. Suddenly nothing she had done over the past week made sense. Why had she resisted him? Why did she have to be so stubborn? All this self-discipline was exhausting. It made her heart and her head ache. Why hadn't she given in days ago, when there was still time?

*Because,* she reminded herself, *it wasn't practical then and it's still not practical now.*

When he finally released her, she took a moment to catch her breath. She had to regain her footing. Had to regain control.

"So," she asked, hoping she sounded sarcastic rather than insecure, "is there someone at the other end waiting for you to do this to her?"

"No."

"Why not?"

"Because I'm a terrible kisser."

"Yeah, you are." She took a step back and pulled on her sunglasses to keep her eyes from betraying her. "You'd better go. Bye."

Thorsten caught her arm as she turned. "I'll see you in June."

"I don't know. Maybe."

"Shannon—"

"I don't know. Maybe." She didn't have the strength to negotiate. Her head hurt.

"Why do you have to be so tough? I'm not so bad, am I? I never called you Bossy Cow once."

"What? Who told you—"

He kissed her once more, lightly. "I'll see you in June. Don't kiss anyone but me until then."

"Maybe." Her lips felt thick with the blood pumping through them. Her head felt thick, too—slow and dull-witted. *Say something. Don't act so loopy. End with the upper hand.*

"I don't normally let people stay in my house, Thorsten. It's a pretty big test—try not to mess up."

"You'll see," he answered. "I am a very reliable boarder."

He squeezed her hand and finally let her go. Shannon turned and resisted looking back.

Safe in her car she leaned against the steering wheel and tried to muster her senses. Since when did a man have an effect like that on her? When was the last time a simple kiss could throw her like that? It wasn't just a simple kiss, though —it was everything behind it. It was the full force of what Thorsten was promising, if only she would give in.

Shannon couldn't remember the last time she felt so unsteady, so unsure of herself. And lurking in her heart somewhere was a strange almost girlish giddiness that she could still feel this way. *Brilliant, Shan. Next thing you know, you'll be dotting your i's with little hearts.*

She had a trial beginning in two weeks—an ugly shareholder dispute where the verdict could move millions for her client.

What were the chances her foggy brain would clear in time?

NORMALLY HER HOUSE in Minneapolis was a cozy refuge, but it felt cold after her time in Arizona. Spring was still resisting the calendar. Shannon dropped her luggage on the kitchen floor and walked straight to the thermostat.

When she returned to the kitchen she found the first note.

RECIPE FOR ICELANDIC TOAST: 2 SLICES BREAD, 2 SLICES CHEESE, APRICOT JAM, THINK OF ME.

Several jars of apricot jam sat lined up on the counter. Shannon opened the refrigerator and found a package of deli-sliced baby Swiss. And that wasn't all: A package of smoked salmon, a bowl of tossed salad, and a covered casserole dish. Shannon lifted the lid. Artichoke hearts and crab meat in a creamy cheese soufflé.

Shannon read the accompanying note. BAKE 30 MINUTES, EAT, THINK OF ME.

*As if you have to remind me.* She had barely thought of anything or anyone else the past few days. When she closed her eyes she could still feel that last long kiss. Her lips had ached for hours afterward. Her body echoed with unfulfilled yearning. Was she wrong to have held back? What would it have hurt?

*Me.*

*The love fest is over, Shan. Time to get back to work.*

She popped the casserole in the oven and hauled her luggage upstairs. She played back her messages—fourteen of them, half from her office. They could wait another day. She wasn't scheduled to be at her desk until tomorrow morning.

E-mails next. A hundred and thirty-seven. She scrolled through the addresses—nothing from Thorsten. She hadn't really expected one from him this soon, but it didn't hurt to check.

*You're acting like a teenager. Snap out of it, litigator. You've got work to do.*

She changed into sweatpants and a sweatshirt and thick wool socks. Then reluctantly she carried her briefcase downstairs and set it beside her plush reading chair. She poured a glass of merlot and settled in to work.

Half an hour later she still sat staring into space. The files lay unread on her lap. A rich aroma wafted from the kitchen. Shannon gave up the pretense of working and gave in to Thorsten's call.

She could feel him there. Carrying in the groceries, moving around her kitchen, tossing this salad, assembling this soufflé. She ate slowly, in no hurry to be done with the memory of him.

She couldn't help herself. She sat at the long dining room table imagining what it would be like to have him there. Imagined clinking their glasses together, eating this succulent meal, smiling across the table at each other, knowing what would come next. They might sit for a while on the couch, Thorsten rubbing the cold from her feet, Shannon bending forward every so often to kiss his appealing mouth.

"Let's go upstairs," he would say.

They would link arms and...

*Ugh. Get a grip. This is pathetic!*

She stacked the dishes in the sink and returned to her reading chair. She tried to focus on the deposition outlines her assistant had prepared and on the various motions she would have to argue in the coming week. None of it excited her. None of it mattered. All she wanted to do was kiss him again...

*Oh, really? That's all you want to do with him? Since when?*

She groaned and flicked off the light. She would be better focused in the morning, she told herself. *Get it out of your system. Go to bed and think whatever you want, but tomorrow wake up and be done.*

*At least for now. At least until June.*

But he was there again in the morning. There in her underwear drawer.

NICE PANTIES. ARE YOU THINKING OF ME?

Shannon laughed out loud. Why hadn't she done something about him? Why had she let him go?

In the pockets of her suits, her pants, her overcoat—more notes crumpling against her hand over the next several days. YOU MISS ME, DON'T YOU?...YOU WISH YOU COULD KISS ME AGAIN...And her favorite, DON'T YOU WISH WE WERE DRINKING HOT CHOCOLATE BESIDE THE FIRE? She did wish that—all of it. She wished she could come home after work and find him here. She wished they slept in the same bed every night. She wished...

The trial came and went. Another one loomed in the coming weeks. How many more days until Iceland? How many until Thorsten?

Yet still he didn't write. Nor did she. It was more of their game, she supposed—waiting for the other to give in first.

April, May, June. End of June. Like the fallacy of nine months' pregnancy—the baby comes at the end, not the beginning of the ninth month. June had to pass through its first three long weeks before she could step onto a plane and go find out what would happen next.

DO YOU MISS ME?

*Every day, and you know it. The question is, are you missing me? Or is there someone there who keeps you warm at night? Are you kissing someone right now? Or are you waiting for me?*

June 25. Saturday. Backpack loaded, ready for adventure.

Heart unsteady, wondering if it was ready for the same.

6

Thorsten had forgotten. No, not forgotten, he thought, just not thoroughly remembered. She was this beautiful. She emerged from Annie's car wearing black hiking pants and a blue fleece jacket and those soft brown curls he had run his fingers through when he shampooed her hair in camp and those grayish-green eyes that could look halfway into his soul and that smile that cut through him like a skiff over the waves, and even though he had practiced his opening line a dozen times that morning it still sounded terrible.

"Hello, Sugarplum, did you miss me?"

Shannon's eyes narrowed and her smile toughened into a smirk. "Like a rash."

Wrong approach. He should have tried sincerity instead of bravado.

So many times in the past two months he had written her e-mails, and each time he deleted them before he could send them. What could he say? What did she really know about him, or him about her? Writing to her might have laid that foundation, but he could never get the words just right. Everything sounded too serious or too boring. She hadn't written to him, either—maybe for all the same reasons. What he really needed was to see her again—to give both of them a chance to discover who they really were. They had both offered hints of themselves in Tucson, but Thorsten knew how much he had held back, and could only assume Shannon had done the same.

"*Góðan dag*," he greeted his sister-in-law, giving her a peck on the cheek.

"*Góðan dag*," Annie replied.

"Your accent has gotten much better," he told her.

"Kjartan has been working with me."

Thorsten winked. "I hope so." It was so much easier to focus on Annie. Shannon still stood on the other side of the car, waiting—for what?

This wasn't how he pictured it. She was supposed to run to him—all right, maybe not run, but at least walk with purpose. She would be so anxious to see him she would wrap him in her arms and pull his mouth to hers, and eventually Annie would have to pry them apart because the customers were complaining.

Thorsten squinted toward the shore of Breidafjördur Bay. Five people clustered on the grassy headland. "There's the rest of the group down there. That tall one is Ólaf—he's guiding with me. He'll give you your tent and your kayaking gear. The others are Elin and Tinna—they're the women on the left—and the couple is Halldor and Mari."

"Are they all Icelandic?" Annie asked.

"All of us but you."

"Good," Annie said. "I can work on my vocabulary."

"They all speak English," Thorsten told Shannon. "Don't worry."

"I'm not worried." She peered at him with an expression he wasn't sure how to interpret.

"Okay, so..." Thorsten hesitated, unsure exactly what to do or say next. "Then you can go down and meet the others. I have to bring more gear. I'll be down soon." He headed toward the weather-worn, boarded up farmhouse on the property. Thorsten's company had an arrangement with the owner to use his shed for storing their kayaks and camping gear.

"Do you need any help?" Annie called after him.

*Plenty. Can you turn back the clock and let me start over? Can you rip out my tongue and beat me over the head with it?* "No, it's okay. I'll be there in a minute."

He strode toward the supply shed cursing himself. What had happened just then? Why was it all so awkward? And how could he get back on trail?

"Thorsten."

Shannon caught up with him at the door to the wooden shed.

"Annie didn't say anything about it, so I wanted to settle with you. I don't want her paying for this—it's my treat." She handed him a credit card. "Okay?"

This wasn't at all like he imagined it. "Uh...no, don't worry about it." He pushed the card away.

"Well, you're not paying for it, either." She thrust her card forward again. "I'm serious—take it."

Thorsten sighed. He glanced toward shore. Annie had joined the others. Ólaf was showing all of them how to set up their tents.

"Come here," Thorsten said. He opened the door to the supply shed and gently pulled Shannon inside.

Thorsten closed the door. It was easier to talk in the dark.

"Let me try this again. Hello, Shannon."

She hesitated. "Hello."

"I missed you very much. I thought about you all the time. I'm so glad you're here."

Shannon didn't answer.

Thorsten reached for her.

"Don't—" She pulled away. "I can't—I'm not—I don't know yet what I'm doing here."

They stood only a few inches apart, close enough to hear each other breathing, neither of them touching. It would be so easy to draw her in, but Thorsten resisted.

"I almost didn't come," Shannon continued. "This weekend, I mean. I would have come to Iceland anyway—I mean, you know—to see Annie—but I wasn't sure if I should, you know—"

Shannon groaned. "See? This is part of the problem. I can't form sentences. I've forgotten how to talk. Whenever I'm around you I sound like a—"

Thorsten covered her lips with his own. If neither of them knew what to say, this seemed a better use of their mouths.

The door slammed open.

Ólaf—tall, blond, with a diamond stud in one ear—stood in the doorway. "Wanna come help me," he asked gruffly in Icelandic, "or are you too busy mating in here?"

"Shut the door or I'll tear your liver out," Thorsten answered in kind.

"How long you gonna leave me alone with these people? That guy Halldor's a real ass."

"You need to work on your client skills," Thorsten told him. He switched to English. "Shannon, this is Ólaf."

Ólaf nodded to her. "Think you're done with him, miss? I could use some help."

"Ólaf..." Thorsten warned.

Shannon stepped away from Thorsten and ducked past Ólaf out the door. "Sorry, I—sorry. He's all yours." She was gone before Thorsten could stop her.

"You're the ass," Thorsten growled.

Ólaf grinned and chomped his gum. "She's a real honey. That other one, too. Sisters?"

"Hands off. They're both taken."

"Did you see that look she gave me? She thinks I'm your boss."

"Let's fix that." Thorsten gathered a load of paddles and hoisted them onto Ólaf's shoulder. "You carry. I'll supervise."


So far, so wrong, Shannon thought as she escaped down the hill. This wasn't the way she had rehearsed it. In her version Thorsten came toward her the minute he saw her and folded her into his arms. He whispered things like, "When can I get you alone?" and "I've missed you so much," and "Shannon, I can't believe you're here"—just like he had in the shed. Remarkably, despite their rocky beginning, Thorsten had done his part.

She, in turn, was supposed to answer, "I'm just here for the weekend," and "It will never work," and "I'm just here because Annie asked me—don't make too much of it."

She had blown her lines. Everything was going all right—she had her game face on, Thorsten was keeping his distance—then he had to pull her into the shed. And kiss her like that. And it was better than she remembered it—quite a feat, since she had replayed those scenes at the airport and that night outside camp a hundred times over the past two months. But memory was unreliable—ask any witness she had ever torn apart on the stand—and seeing him again, feeling his body and his mouth and smelling his skin and hearing his voice and wishing she knew him better and could spend more of her life discovering him than just these few days—all that was real. Those were the facts.

If Ólaf hadn't burst in on them, who knows how far she would have taken it? Tackled him to the floor and ripped both their clothes down to skin and muscled him into—

"Shan." Annie waved her hand in front of her cousin's face. "You okay?"

Shannon nodded. She turned her attention to the group in front of her. "Hi. I'm—" *A hopeless school girl in love with your guide. I haven't a brain in my head right now because he just kissed me and I forgot how much I liked that and needed that and won't you all excuse me now while I go back up the hill and find him and take him off somewhere secluded so we can—*

"Do you live here, too?" asked the brunette named Tinna.

"Uh, no. I'm just visiting. I live in Minnesota, in the U.S." From the corner of her eye she spied Thorsten and Ólaf descending the hill.

"I've been there," said Tinna's friend Elin, a blond woman in her mid-thirties. "I was there last year."

Shannon was grateful to find something safe to talk about. The other Icelanders mentioned places they had visited—New York, Chicago, Disneyworld.

"Is this your first time in Iceland?" Tinna wanted to know.

"First of many," Annie answered for her. "I hope she'll come visit me often."

"Tell them the truth," Thorsten prompted.

"What...truth?" Shannon asked warily.

"She came to see me. She's hoping to win my love."

Shannon choked out a laugh. "What?"

"She's crazy about me," Thorsten continued. "She's been writing to me for months, begging me to see her again. So I charged her double to come on this trip."

The other guests seemed to enjoy this preliminary entertainment. Annie in particular had a merry glint in her eye.

*So, Thorsten, that's how you want to play it.* The challenge had been made: Who could outdo the other in nonchalance?

"It's true," Shannon said. "I'm here to propose."

"This all sounds very important," said Halldor, a portly man in his forties, "but do you think we can get on with it? I've been standing here an hour. I paid to kayak, not listen to mating calls."

Shannon admired Thorsten's smooth transition. He smiled pleasantly. "Has anyone here ever kayaked before?"

"Ólaf already asked us that," Halldor answered.

Ólaf rolled his eyes.

"I like to ask again," said Thorsten. "Ólaf's a little deaf."

"Yes, we're beginners—all of us," barked Halldor. "Don't know about your lady here."

"Good," Thorsten said, ignoring this last comment, "then none of you will have any bad habits we need to fix. First we'll put up the tents, then eat lunch, then we paddle."

Grumbling at yet another delay—"You'd think for the money they'd put up the tents for us"—Halldor led his wife to the nearest plot of flat grassland. Tinna and Elin chose a tent site a few yards away, and Annie and Shannon took the furthest spot.

"What was all that about?" Annie asked Shannon.

"I don't know—that Halldor's a piece of work."

"I meant between you and Thorsten."

"Oh. Nothing. We're just playing."

"And what were you doing in the shed?" Annie smiled mischievously. "More playing?"

"Mind your own business."

"This is definitely my business. I'm an old married woman now. I live for you young people's romances."

Slowly all three army-green tents began to take shape. The wind, which had until then been a mere annoyance, whipped into tent-snapping gusts that threatened to blow everyone's shelters into the sea. While the clients struggled with their smaller structures, Thorsten and Ólaf battled with the kitchen-sized dining tent.

"How cold do you think it is?" Shannon asked.

"I don't know—maybe forty." Annie squinted up at the sky. "When it's cloudy like this, it can feel pretty chilly."

"Is it like this a lot?"

"More days than not." Annie shrugged. "But then when the sun's out, it's especially nice. How would you know what you were missing if it was like that all the time?"

Shannon shook her head. "This from the woman who used to complain if it rained more than two days in a row."

"It must be love," Annie answered.

"Must be."

As soon as they had staked out the edges of their tent, Shannon and Annie dove inside for some relief from the biting wind. They blew on their fingers and rubbed their hands together.

The tent had two separate compartments: a sleeping area with room for two sleeping bags and a small enclosed vestibule for storage of luggage or packs.

"Should we bring in the rest of the stuff now?" Annie asked.

"Might as well. I need to find my gloves before my fingers break off."

They streaked up the hill toward Annie's car, retrieved their gear, and dove back inside the relative warmth of their tent. The wind slapped against the nylon walls and shook the poles.

"We need to move the stakes and guy out the tent a little better," Shannon said. "Look how it's already drooping."

"Have you ever camped in wind like this?" Annie asked.

"I don't think so—not this bad."

They had just finished organizing their gear and laying out their sleeping bags when Thorsten poked his head through the tent flap.

"Lunch time. All set in here?" He cocked an eyebrow at Shannon. "Last chance—sure you don't want to share a tent with me instead of Annie?"

"Fairly certain, thanks."

"I'm much warmer," Thorsten argued.

"And much too friendly," answered Shannon. "Did you make that offer to the others?"

"Yes, and so far you're the only one who said no."

"Well, then, I don't feel so bad." She crawled toward the tent door and began zipping Thorsten out. "We have to change. See you in a bit."

Thorsten appealed to Annie. "You know, she's crazy about me."

"You keep saying that," Annie answered as Thorsten's face disappeared behind the zipper. She waited until he was out of range before whispering to Shannon, "And I'd say he's right."

"Say whatever you want, but I know I'm just here to have fun with my cousin."

"Uh-huh."

"Besides," Shannon added, "one convert in the family is enough. If the Icelanders take any more of our women it'll become an international incident."

They changed into warmer layers and strode toward the dining tent. They ducked under the flaps, leaving the snapping wind behind, welcoming the warmth of the propane heater and the assembled crowd.

The tent housed two long tables, one for food preparation, one for dining. Canvas chairs horseshoed around the tables. Two folding loveseats made up a second row of chairs, closer to the tent walls.

Plastic bins filled with packaged and fresh food sat at the far end of the tent, along with the propane heater, a propane stove, several plastic water jugs, and assorted cooking supplies.

The scent of strong coffee hung in the warm air. "Ah, that's what I need," sighed Shannon. The other guests sat already sipping from steaming mugs. Thorsten poured coffee for the cousins, who then settled onto one of the love seats and leaned against each other for added warmth.

Thorsten and Ólaf distributed information packets and liability forms. Thorsten was uncommonly sober as he explained the risks of kayaking in open water, in seas so cold even a short dunking could prove lethal. "We all stay together, right? If one of you falls in, we have to be able to get to you fast." He paused for effect. "But no one falls in, right? We'll teach you that part after lunch. Let's eat."


THE DAY WAS PERFECT. Well, maybe too windy, Thorsten thought, but at least the sky was clear again so Shannon could see how beautiful it was there.

He admired her athleticism. He had already observed her strength while backpacking, but she proved to be a strong paddler as well. Thorsten and Ólaf paddled single-man kayaks at the front and back of the group while the guests paddled in pairs. Shannon and Annie were the strongest team by far. They worked together well establishing a steady, spirited pace, then taking rest breaks when they needed. Elin and Tinna were slow but stable. It was Mari and Halldor who had trouble from the beginning. She was too tentative and he was too critical. Thorsten stayed at the rear with them, encouraging Mari and striving to tolerate her husband.

Thorsten paused to watch Shannon stroke across the waves. What was she thinking? Here she was, her first trip to Iceland, her first time paddling in the ocean. Her first time seeing him since they kissed goodbye at the airport. He had played the scene back countless times—the look in her eyes, the warm invitation of her mouth, the way she had responded to him while at the same time pretending not to care. But she did care. He could see it now, too, in the way she glanced at him shyly in the dining tent, the way she had responded to him in the shed. He wanted to believe she was just waiting, the way he was, for a time when they could be alone. And then what? What should he say? Should he keep it light and fun, or try to move beyond where they last left off?

"Good, Mari," Thorsten shouted in Icelandic. "You're doing well."

"I'm tired!" she called.

"I don't see why," Halldor griped. "I'm doing most of the paddling."

"We'll stop just ahead," Thorsten promised her. "See that island up there?"

Mari puffed out a sigh and renewed her efforts.

"Good, Mari, that's it," Thorsten said. "Try to match her

strokes," he reminded her husband. Halldor grimaced and paddled harder, paying no attention to the pace his wife set.

Thorsten hated men like that. He saw them all the time on trips like this. They were the ones who stomped off ahead on hiking trips, then waited impatiently for their spouses or girlfriends to catch up. They were the ones who ridiculed their mates' slow but honest progress, never satisfied by anything less than perfection.

The couple's kayak stuttered across the waves. "Just a little further," Thorsten encouraged. "Come on, that's it."

"I need a better front motor," Halldor sneered.

"I'll get you one," Thorsten answered.

He had just the right person in mind.

7

___________

They pulled onto the shore of one of the small islands. Spongy moss covered the foundation of black lava rock. Shannon sprang across the ground as though pacing across the moon.

From the pocket of his hull Ólaf removed two dry bags filled with food and drink. "We have sandwiches, coffee, " he announced in English, "also nuts and cookies."

Shannon sampled the Icelandic version of trail mix—salty dates mixed with nuts and chocolate candies—and downed a cup of half coffee, half cocoa. The wind had died down some, but the air was still chilled. Shannon's fingers burned with cold. The sailing gloves she had worn while paddling were soaked from the icy sea. But the spray skirt and waterproof jacket Ólaf had supplied kept her torso warm, and the combination of her fleece neck gaiter and hat preserved much of her body heat. If she had worn diving booties instead of her boots, she might be perfectly content despite the pool of water in the bottom of their kayak that kept dousing her feet.

"What do you think?" she asked Annie.

"Hard work, but nice. It's beautiful out here."

"Does anything live on these islands?" Shannon asked Ólaf.

"Eider ducks. And those birds you see up there. They're called *kriyas*. They're very mean."

"Mean how?" Annie asked.

"They'll come after you if you get too close to their nests." He simulated an attack, screeching and clawing at the air. He rapped on his head. "That's why I wear a helmet. Keeps my brain from getting pecked out."

Shannon and Annie exchanged a look. "*The Birds,*" Shannon pronounced ominously.

Ólaf nodded. "Hitchcock? *Já.* Like that."

Thorsten was avoiding her. He kept busy appearing busy, but Shannon could see he wasn't really doing much.

When he finally did look at her, it was to motion for her to follow him. She kept her expression neutral as she rose and brushed off her clothes.

He drew her away only a short distance, still within sight of the others. "I need a favor," he said.

"Okay."

"Halldor is a bastard."

She laughed. "Okay."

"I would like Mari to have a good time."

"That's nice of you."

"So I would like you to switch partners," he concluded.

"You want me to go with Mari?"

"No, with Halldor."

She smiled wickedly. "Hm...all right. That could be fun."

"Good. Thank you. Now can I show you something?"

Shannon looked back at the group. Only Annie seemed to be watching. "Okay."

She followed him over a mild swell in the island and dropped onto the other side, out of the wind and out of sight of the others. Banks of pink flowers lined the course to the sea.

"Over here," Thorsten said. He knelt beside a shallow indentation.

Still standing, Shannon peered over his shoulder at the empty nest. A few shells lay broken nearby.

"Eider ducks," Thorsten said. He held up a clump of soft white down. When she reached for it he clasped her hand and pulled her down beside him.

Their mouths instantly found each other. Thorsten pulled her in, his cold hands sliding up the back of her kayaking jacket.

"Ah, Shannon, I missed you," Thorsten whispered.

She smothered his words. She gave up breathing for the moment. She did not want to waste a second—they could breathe or talk any time. Right now all she wanted was to taste him.

"I have to go back," he said too soon.

"Yep. Okay." One more hungry kiss. Then Shannon sat back on her heels to gather her scattered wits. She noticed she wasn't cold any more. "Okay," she repeated, signaling her legs to stand.

Thorsten held out his hand and pulled her up. He strode ahead a few paces and called to group, "Everybody ready?"

*Sure—just give me an hour,* Shannon thought. She followed on shaky legs. How did he have this power to turn her body and her mind to putty?

*Regroup, Shan. Pull up. Repeat after me: This will never work.*

By the time she joined the group Thorsten had already reassigned the paddlers: Annie with Elin, Mari with Tinna, Shannon with Halldor.

Halldor looked her over. "Do you want the bow or stern?"

Her lips felt too swollen to talk. "Uh, I'll take the bow," Shannon answered.

"You just don't want to get your feet wet," he said.

That snapped her out of her reverie. She smiled sweetly as she climbed into the front of the craft. "That's right," she said. "I'm terribly delicate."

Halldor waded through the water to push off. He climbed in with a grunt.

Shannon set her paddle. "Ready?"


THORSTEN WATCHED WITH GROWING ADMIRATION. This was even better than he predicted.

He knew she must be tired. The wind had kicked up again and seemed to push the paddlers back one stroke for every two. The waters were choppy and the kayakers fought against the tide.

She was magnificent.

While Halldor grunted and swore and only pretended to paddle at times, Shannon dug the blades of her paddle into the water and motored the kayak forward at impressive speed. She barely rested. She set a blistering rhythm, then dared Halldor to match it. After a short time, he didn't even try.

"Come on, Halldor!" Shannon shouted. "Paddle! That shore isn't coming to us!"

He answered with an Icelandic curse.

"What does that mean?" Shannon asked Thorsten, who paddled nearby.

"'To the devil with you.' It's very bad."

"Halldor!" Shannon scolded. "We're partners. Come on now—stroke! Stroke!"

At one point the taunts proved too much for him. Halldor leaned forward and dug his paddle through the waves with all his might. The short burst of power propelled them forward into the unrelenting wind.

"Good!" Shannon shouted. "Keep going!"

But the burst was brief. Soon Halldor gasped for air and Shannon paddled alone once again.

She pulled her paddle from the water and laid it across the bow. "I can't do this alone," she told Halldor.

"I'm tired."

"I'm tired, too."

Thorsten paddled closer. "Do you need a pull?"

"No," Halldor spat in Icelandic. "Why don't you go some-place else?"

Thorsten, too, switched to their native tongue. "We have to stay together for safety," he reminded Halldor, then he gestured toward Shannon. "Strong, isn't she?"

"*Já*," Halldor answered surlily.

"A woman like that can be dangerous, don't you think?"

Halldor offered his opinion in Icelandic, then switched back to English for Shannon's benefit. "Does your superior know you brought your girlfriend on this trip?"

"Oh, she's not my girlfriend. We only met today."

"That's true," Shannon agreed.

Halldor huffed. "I saw the two of you on that island."

"Hm," Thorsten answered. "Are you ready to paddle again?"

They nosed onto shore just behind Mari and Tinna, who had benefited from a slow steady pace throughout. Annie and Elin followed a few minutes later, with Ólaf bringing up the rear.

Thorsten pulled his kayak onto shore, then tugged the others up beside it with their crews still inside. No one seemed anxious to stand.

When finally Shannon did emerge from the kayak she turned to Halldor and offered her hand. "That was great. Thanks, Halldor. Good job."

This was apparently too much for him. He wriggled out of his hole and stumbled onto shore. "I'll speak to your superior," he threatened Thorsten. "I'm sure he wants to know what you do on these trips."

"Ólaf is my superior," Thorsten answered. "Speak to him if you like."

Thorsten dragged the empty kayak further up the sand. Shannon picked up one end and helped him carry it up to the grass. Then she set it down and stood beside him facing the water. They kept their voices low.

"That nearly killed me," she said. "I can't lift my arms."

"I know, but you were spectacular," Thorsten murmured. "Thank you—that was just what I wanted."

"Will you get in trouble?"

"No."

"Is Ólaf really your superior?"

Thorsten grinned. "Sure. And I am his."

"So what's going to happen?"

"Let him yell about me for a while. Ólaf knows what to do."

Shannon dropped her voice to a whisper. "We should be more careful."

"No. We should do whatever we like. I guarantee Halldor will leave tonight."

He reached for the tips of Shannon's fingers and squeezed them.

"You, I hope, are staying."

8

"So, obviously you two are picking up where you left off," Annie said.

"No. I don't know. I'm not sure."

"Maybe you should take Thorsten up on his offer to share a tent."

"No, thanks. In fact, I need to talk to you about something."

Annie smiled and rubbed her palms together. "Oh, good."

Shannon leaned back on her sleeping bag. An early evening squall beat against their tent. Thorsten and Ólaf were in the dining tent making dinner. Tinna and Elin were resting in their tent. As predicted, Halldor and Mari had already left.

"I'm not sure what to do about backpacking," Shannon confessed. "Thorsten hasn't mentioned it, and I'm not sure I want to go."

"But you brought all your backpacking gear—I saw it."

"I know. I wanted to be ready if I decided. But I haven't decided."

Annie leaned back on her elbow and faced her cousin. "I think there are some elementary principles you need to work out."

"Spoken like a teacher."

"First, you're in Iceland."

"Yes. That's true."

"Second, you love to backpack."

"True."

"Third, you're in love with Thorsten."

"Sshh!" Shannon sat up and hugged her knees to her chest. "That's not true at all."

"Shan, you've been fighting this since my wedding. It's just us. No one can hear. It doesn't mean you have to do anything about it—just tell me. It is the truth, isn't it?"

Shannon groaned and lay back down. "Look. It's a ridiculous situation."

"Why ridiculous?"

"He lives here, I don't. I live there, he doesn't. That seems pretty concrete."

"I did it," Annie said.

"That's you. That's Kjartan. That's true love if I ever saw it. It doesn't work that way for me."

"Why not?"

"Because I'm different."

"How?"

Shannon held up her left hand and pointed to her ring finger. "Remember? Jewelry doesn't want to stay on this finger."

"Erik was a mistake."

"Yeah, well, I'm awfully good at making mistakes."

Annie groaned. "You're so stupid sometimes."

"Spoken like a true romantic. May the witness be excused?"


TINNA RETURNED from her excursion to the latrine and poked her head into the dining tent. "The sun is out. Come see."

It was 11:30 at night. The group had lingered over dinner—pasta with salmon and vegetables, wine, cheese, chocolate cake, coconut cookies, more wine. The tent offered warm comfort from the wind. The rain had drizzled to a stop a few hours before. Now, as Tinna discovered, the sun had emerged in full force. It shone like noon.

"Let's move out there," Thorsten suggested.

Shannon was reluctant to lose her position beside him. She liked the feeling of his leg pressing against hers beneath the table. When his hand slipped onto her knee she left it there, even though every touch was torture. Her conversation with Annie hadn't helped. She still hadn't sorted through what to do next. For now she resolved not to think about any of it.

The group transferred chairs outside and carefully carried the table laden with wine and cheese and crackers. For the next half hour they pretended the sun cancelled the cold. They leaned back in their chairs and soaked up the light. They reached for crackers with stiff, trembling fingers and chewed with chattering teeth.

"Okay, I'm freezing," Annie finally admitted. "I have to go back inside."

The spell broken, the rest of the party retreated with her.

As Shannon was about to slip through the flap of the tent, Thorsten caught her arm.

"Come for a walk with me? I want to show you something."

*Say no.* "All right."

They climbed the hill behind the dining tent, past an outdoor sink that pumped fresh water from the nearby spring, onto level ground that paralleled the road.

Thorsten pointed to the black peak in front of them. "That's Gottfell—Good Mountain. It's good luck to climb it, but you have to do it right. There are three special rules. First, you have to climb before sundown—we have plenty of time. Second, once you start up, you can't look behind— that's very important. And third... " He hesitated. "Maybe I'll tell you when we get to the top. Want to go?"

"Okay."

They scaled the black mountain in silence. Shannon followed Thorsten's lead up the thin track. Their boots crunched on loose rock. So strange, Shannon thought, to be hiking with him again in a place so radically different. They were different, too. They had taken their first cautious steps toward knowing each other, and now, it seemed, they stood part way up the mountain. Where the rest of the climb might lead her, Shannon did not know. But she was willing to keep walking for now.

When they reached the top, Thorsten said, "Now you can look back."

She looked back down the steep trail, then shifted her eyes to the ocean. From up here she could see most of the islands where they had kayaked. The colors were beautiful— wild flowers and rich green grass clinging to black rock. Beyond the islands lay open sea, then Greenland, then America. So far to go, she reminded herself. Thorsten lived in another world entirely.

The wind was stronger up here. It cut through her jacket and pricked at her skin. Shannon crossed her arms over her chest.

"Cold?"

She nodded. Thorsten stepped forward and wrapped his arms around her.

It was exactly what she had wanted, even though she didn't know it until that moment. She wanted to be safe with him. To give up the cleverness and the stolen moments and rest instead in the comfort of his arms.

Shannon laid her cheek against his chest. She waited for the shivers to subside.

"The stories say there are elves inside this mountain," Thorsten told her. "They watch as you climb, and if you do everything right, they will tell the mountain to grant you one wish."

She lifted her head. "You said there were three things you had to do."

"Go before sundown," Thorsten recited, "don't look behind, and..." He met her eyes, then gently pushed her head back against his chest. "And take along someone who holds a piece of your heart."

Shannon's own heart thundered in her chest. "Thorsten—"

"So I thought, who can I bring?" he continued lightly. "Halldor? No. Ólaf? Already done that."

"You have."

"Of course. But it only works once. You have to bring someone different every time."

"How many people have you brought here?"

"About fifty."

Shannon lifted her head again. "Good. I feel much better now."

Thorsten warmed her lips with a kiss that traveled through her veins like flames.

It was worse than being a teenager. There was no reason to hold back—no one was going to punish them, she was on birth control and knew all the necessary precautions—and yet she knew she couldn't let it happen. The only thing stopping her from fulfilling this marrow-deep need was her own reckless sense of self-preservation. She wished there were another reason to tell him no, but nothing convenient presented itself.

She drew away. Pressed against him again. Drew away once more.

She ducked her head and tried to clear it. "Thorsten..."

He stroked her arm. "Shannon..."

She peered into his bright, questioning eyes. "I have to sit down."

She plopped onto the trail and rested her head in her hands. The wind whipped at her unmercifully. Thorsten sat beside her. "Can you put your arm around me?" she asked. "I'm freezing."

He pulled her into a sturdy embrace. "Better?"

Shannon nodded. She knew she should say something, but she couldn't think what that might be.

Thorsten said it for her. "You think it's too fast."

"Yes."

"I say things about my heart, but all you want to do is sleep with me."

Shannon's teeth chattered into a laugh. "Keep dreaming."

Thorsten kissed the top of her head. "I think about you every day."

Shannon gulped down her reply. She could say too much here. *Be strong. Keep it light.*

"Thanks for all the notes. It made getting dressed in the morning a lot more fun."

Thorsten seemed to accept the message she was sending. He sat silently for a while, keeping her close.

In time he told her, "We should go back down. Did you make your wish?"

The implication was clear: that he knew he held a piece of her heart as well. Shannon decided not to argue. "What do these elves look like?"

"We're not allowed to say. If you lived here, you'd know."

"Will they accept a wish from a foreigner?"

"Yes," Thorsten answered, "but only if you believe in elves."

Shannon shut her eyes tightly. *Why not?* she thought as she made her wish. *Maybe an elf will take pity on me. I certainly can't come up with a solution myself.*

"Done," she said.

Thorsten stood and helped her up. Her legs had stiffened again. "My whole body is one ache," she confessed. "I practically killed myself showing off for Halldor."

"Do you know what he told Ólaf?"

"No."

"He said I shouldn't be allowed to bring my girlfriend just so she could mate with me in the grass and then humiliate the clients by proving she was a better paddler than any of them."

"Wow, that's quite a compliment—except for the mating part. What did Ólaf say?"

"That Halldor must be mistaken, since company policy is that we mate only on the rocks and only with weak women."

Shannon laughed. "I guess Halldor wasn't very impressed with that answer."

"I guess not."

"What will happen?" Shannon asked. "Do you have to give him his money back?"

"Probably. It doesn't matter."

"Ólaf isn't really your boss, is he? Won't someone be mad?"

"No. I made my wish tonight. Everything will be all right."

"What did you wish?"

Thorsten clicked his tongue. "If you tell, the elves won't grant it."

"These elves have a lot of rules."

"Of course. They hold all the power."

They scuttered down the trail and back onto the grasslands. Thorsten reached for her hand as he had done on their walk to the ice cream parlor. All the emotions of that night rushed through once more—the feeling of trust, of tenderness, of passion that burned so deeply it threatened to consume all the barriers she had defended for so long.

As they neared the dining tent, Thorsten said, "I was serious, you know—about sharing my tent. Ólaf can sleep in the kitchen."

Shannon stopped and looked him in the eye. *You know I want to,* she almost said, but settled for, "I can't. I'm here with Annie."

"Annie will understand."

"I don't think I do." She squeezed his hand. "I'm tired. I have to go to bed. I'll see you in the morning." She left him and walked on to the dining tent. She leaned in and said good night.

Annie followed her out. "Good. I'm so tired, but I didn't want to leave yet—I'm having too much fun." She glanced back as Thorsten entered the dining tent. "Anything happen?"

"You are the nosiest—"

"Should I expect someone throwing rocks at your window tonight?"

Shannon laced her arm through her cousin's. "It's so easy for you married women—you've forgotten what it's like out here in the real world."

"Iceland is hardly the real world—trust me."

They ducked inside their tent and zipped out the wind. Shannon stripped to her long underwear and dove inside her sleeping bag. She shivered, knowing the cold night was only partially to blame.

He appeared with two mugs of coffee and a report about Ólaf's snoring. "It could strip the feathers off a duck."

"Thanks," Shannon said, wrapping her cold fingers around the mug. "How's the weather?"

Thorsten looked over his shoulder. "Cloudy, not so much wind as last night."

He looked especially good in the mornings—hair askew, eyes a little droopy, those studious glasses, and always that warm smile when he first laid eyes on her. So far she had been able to hide behind her chaperons—first her brothers, now Annie—but how would she resist him when it was just the two of them alone?

Because she had decided to go backpacking with him. If he asked, she would go.

"Do you think it will rain again?" Annie asked. Another squall had struck during the early morning hours, soaking the already wet clothes Annie and Shannon had foolishly left tied to the outside of their tent.

"Rain is always a good guess," Thorsten answered. "But we won't melt—will we, Shannon?"

Did he mean to look at her that way—stripping away any pretense and laying bare his attraction for anyone to see?

Shannon's eyes narrowed briefly, mirroring the lust in Thorsten's gaze. *So much for detachment,* she thought. *Damn, that man is handsome.*

"No, I won't melt." She smiled guiltily as she glanced away.

"I don't know about you two," Annie said, "but my arms feel like they were pinned under a truck all night." She rubbed her shoulder. "I don't know how much I have in me today."

"We won't go out so far this time," Thorsten assured her. "We'll be finished by lunch. Ólaf will be ready with breakfast soon. We should be going."

"How come you've let Ólaf do all the cooking?" Shannon asked. "I was looking forward to some of your meals."

"Don't worry, I'll cook for you..."

*"I'll cook for you." Was that an invitation?*

"...but Ólaf has to learn how to impress women with his cooking, too, you know?"

"Oh, I see," Shannon answered. "And do you think you've impressed me?"

"I know I have. Haven't I, Annie?"

"Don't involve her—"

"Yep," Annie confirmed, "it's all she talks about."

"See?" Thorsten gloated. "I know Annie wouldn't lie. What's her favorite?"

Annie answered before Shannon could stop her. "That hot chocolate you made."

"Okay, good." A stout burst of wind shook the tent. "We have to go soon," Thorsten said. "Come for breakfast."

Annie leaned forward and zipped out the wind. When she turned back her face bore a broad smile.

Shannon squinted sternly. "What?"

"Just admit it," Annie said.

"No."

"You like him *so much.*"

"Mind your own business."

Shannon slid deeper inside her sleeping bag and donned the bra she had stored at the foot of it to keep warm overnight. Nothing shocked the body like strapping on an icy bra first thing in the morning. Roughing it was one thing —torturing oneself unnecessarily was another.

"How are you going to hold up when it's just the two of you out there?" Annie asked. Apparently Annie, too, had decided the issue was settled.

"Fine. I'll do fine. I have my own tent, my own sleeping bag—"

"Your own personal love slave—"

"Nothing's going to happen."

Annie shook her head and smiled maternally. "Poor, poor Shannon. Silly, deluded—"

Shannon wriggled into her fleece pants. "Do you know why nothing is going to happen?"

"No, why?"

"Because I have made it my sworn mission not to let anything happen. This is a test for me. And you know once I decide to win something, it's practically won."

"I do know you're competitive," Annie agreed, "but I think you're outmatched this time. Thorsten is too much what you like in a man. I'd lay money you won't last more than a night."

"How much?" Shannon asked. She zipped up her fleece coat and scooted to the vestibule to begin lacing her boots.

"Nah, money's too easy," Annie said. "How about this? If

I'm right—if you and Thorsten give up this foolishness and actually admit how crazy about each other you are—"

"Easy bet."

"Wait, I'm not finished. If you both admit it and come back from this backpacking trip completely in love, then you owe me a year's nanny service."

Shannon scoffed. "A year? Forget it!" Something in Annie's expression captured Shannon's attention. "Why would you need a nanny service?"

"No reason."

"Annie—"

"I'm not sure yet."

Shannon grinned. "Are you serious?"

"I'm not sure. I wasn't going to say anything—"

Shannon bowled her over in an embrace. "Does Kjartan know?"

Annie's laugh was muffled against Shannon's coat. "Ow! I can't breathe!" When Shannon released her, Annie answered, "I didn't want to tell him until I knew for sure."

Shannon peered into her face. "You look pregnant."

"How would you know?"

"I just do. When are you going to the doctor?"

"Next week," Annie said. "Don't tell Thorsten, all right?"

Shannon swept her finger across her heart. "I promise. So that's the bet, huh? If Thorsten wins me over, I have to come change dirty diapers? Extra incentive not to lose. And if—when—I win, you know what I want?"

"I'm afraid to ask."

"I want to be the fun aunt."

"Actually," Annie said, "I think you'd be the second cousin."

"Whichever. When she's old enough—"

"She could be a boy," Annie reminded her.

Shannon groaned in irritation. "Okay, fine. The point is, I want that child to know I'm the funnest person in the family. You're going to send him or her to me two weeks out of every year so we can ski or backpack or bike or canoe—"

"And what if this child's father doesn't agree?"

"Too bad." Shannon gripped Annie's hand and shook it. "We just made a contract."

"That's all right," Annie said. "I'm not worried. I know exactly what's going to happen. You'll make a great nanny."


SHE MEANT to keep a fair distance from him all day to see if she could clear her head, but the plan dissolved almost right away.

He sat beside her at breakfast, his hand drifting casually under the table to stroke her thigh. All her appetites flooded to a single location. Breakfast lost its appeal.

They stood beside each other on shore assessing the wind and waves.

"We should have slept together last night," Thorsten murmured. "Were you cold, too?" She didn't dare answer.

While the others assembled their gear for the morning's kayak, Thorsten trudged up the hill to the supply shack. He turned back half way and motioned for Shannon to follow. "I want to show you something."

*Show me something.* Her legs followed before her brain could weigh in.

Shannon entered the cold shed. Her eyes barely had time to adjust to the dark when she felt his warm lips on hers. He drew her toward him and slipped his hands beneath her coat. His hands never rose above her belly. Her breasts ached for his touch. She grinded her hips against his and dared him to stop at just a kiss this time.

*What are you doing?*

*Exactly what I want.*

"I have to go down," Thorsten moaned. "Why didn't you sleep with me last night?"

"Because this is a bad idea." She slipped her hands down the back of his pants and pulled him in closer.

"Uh, no, I can't—not now." Thorsten angled his hips away. "I have to go."

"You shouldn't have lured me up here, then."

"I couldn't help it. It's all I think about."

Reluctantly Shannon released him. As one last parting torture Thorsten trailed his finger between her thighs.

"Don't do that," she moaned.

"Come home with me tonight."

"I can't. I'm going with Annie."

"When will you come to me?"

Here it was. Should she wait, play it coy, or plunge ahead?

"I...brought my backpack."

"Thorsten!" Ólaf bellowed from outside. "Let's go, damn you!"

"We have to go. The weather's going to turn—" He stepped toward the door.

"Do you want me to go? Backpacking, I mean?"

He returned and slipped his arm behind her. He pulled her close and whispered in her ear. "Shannon, I want to do whatever you'll let me do. I already told you—you have my heart."

He disappeared through the door without waiting for an answer.

*Back to you, Shan. What's it going to be?*

# 9

*Hobbitsville.* Shannon peered out the bus window at the preternatural green and black hillsides and the long crashing waterfalls bursting from seams in the rocks and understood why Icelanders didn't deny the existence of elves and trolls. She had seen green before, but nothing like this. It was the green of a child's crayon—the exaggerated green you'd find in a slick coffee table book. No one really lived like this, she thought. No one could bear so much beauty every time he threw open the curtains.

Normally she was never sea sick, but the three-hour ferry ride from Stykkishólmur had unsettled her stomach. Following that with a lengthy bus ride from Brjanslækur to Ísafjördur over narrow winding dirt roads hadn't helped. Was it motion sickness or nerves? She visualized their meeting, tried to imagine keeping it light. She would tell him right away that she'd booked a room at the hotel. Then there would be no misunderstanding.

*Who are you trying to kid?* she scolded herself. *What's with all this prudish chastity? He wants you, you want him...*

*It would be more than sex and you know it. You've already lost a chunk of your heart. Hold on to the rest.*

Heavy rain pounded against the bus as it pulled into the outskirts of Ísafjördur. Shannon peered through the fogged window, not quite believing what she saw. Just past the ski lift was a golf course, and at 10:30 at night, under muted sunlight and driving rain, dozens of golfers played as though they couldn't feel a drop. Shannon smiled to herself. She suddenly understood Thorsten's irreverent attitude. Driving rain, driving range—why not? On a nearby field a group of boys kicked around a soccer ball while two young mothers pushed their babies in covered strollers along the sidelines. Few people wore hats, even though it was cold enough to see their breath. As the bus pulled further into town, Shannon wondered if she would see people putting out their sun tea or hanging their laundry on the line.

The oddities provided just the bromide Shannon needed for the butterflies in her stomach. This would be fun—just another adventure. No need to make such a big deal of it.

She saw him through the window as the bus pulled into the parking lot. Shannon drew a deep breath and steadied her nerves. *Be cool. Relax. Have a good time. This doesn't have to mean anything.*

She donned her rain coat and pulled on the hood, then stepped into the chilling shower. Thorsten hesitated, then took a step forward. They stood there awkwardly for a moment, neither making a move.

"Hi," Shannon said.

"Good ride?" Thorsten asked.

"Yeah, it was fine."

The driver greeted Thorsten and chatted in Icelandic while unloading the bags. Shannon was grateful for the distraction. She needed to gather her wits before setting out on this adventure. Not the backpacking trip—that would be easy by comparison. The real risk lay in being alone with Thorsten for so long. She would have to make things clear right away.

Thorsten hoisted her backpack across his shoulders and lifted her carry-on bag. "Ready?"

"Is the hotel far from here?" she asked.

Thorsten looked at her with eyes that seemed to see everything—her conflicting emotions, the great effort she was making to control her attraction to him. She saw what was in his eyes, too—the sharp pain she had just inflicted.

"It's not far," he answered. "Is that where you're staying?"

"Yes."

He nodded. "I hear it's nice. I'll show you."

"I can carry my stuff—"

"You will, starting tomorrow. Did you eat yet?"

"No."

"Good. I made dinner for you."

"Tonight? It's pretty late."

"I never start a hike with a hungry client. You need to eat tonight and then a big breakfast tomorrow. Come with me."

He led her past primly-clean factories and warehouses to a residential block where houses stood shoulder to shoulder behind weather-stripped picket fences and well-kept yards. Yellow houses, red and blue roofs, blooming flowers in pots and beds—the street seemed alive with the colors Shannon imagined the people there must crave during long, dusky winters. The street reminded her of her own in the old section of downtown Minneapolis, with its early-1900 houses and small patches of lawn.

Thorsten approached the only four-story building on the block and turned his key in the lock. "I'm at the top."

The stairwell was clean, although slightly run down with chipping paint and a single burnt out bulb.

"How many other people live here?"

"Only me."

"You're kidding—with all this space? Why?"

"There are better apartments. I got this one cheap."

"How long have you lived here?"

"Ten years."

At the top of the stairs Thorsten turned the knob on his unlocked door and stepped inside. "You can hang your coat there. I'll be back." He carried her pack and bag to a room at the end of the hall.

Shannon stared at the walls. Hundreds—maybe thousands—of photographs lined the hallway. In the hazy light of rain-filled night filtering through the far window, Shannon could see a talent no less masterful than a National Geographer photographer's.

He joined her in the makeshift gallery.

"Thorsten...these are beautiful."

He stood with his arms crossed over his chest. Shannon

was acutely aware they hadn't touched since she stepped from the bus. "Thanks," he answered with a smile. "There's more in there." He pointed to the first room off the hall, across from the small kitchen. "I'll heat up the food. Go ahead and look."

The small bare light bulb beaming from the ceiling in the small room cast shadows that made the photos harder to see. Shannon flipped off the switch and made do with the light coming through the small window.

Purples, lime greens, soft pinks, deep rose—colors she was sure she wouldn't have seen in the rocks and hillsides Thorsten photographed, but which leapt to life under his hands. She shuffled slowly around the room, scanning each photo carefully, taking in the composition and the color, imagining what it might be like to stand under this waterfall or that volcano and see what Thorsten saw.

She glanced through the doorway to where Thorsten moved smoothly about the small kitchen. Pots steamed on the stove. He leaned over the counter chopping and assembling. He looked up and caught her staring.

"Tea?"

"No, thanks," she answered automatically. But tea on a rainy night sounded perfect. "I mean, yeah—that would be good."

She didn't know how to be with him. Before there had always been the safety of other people nearby. Here, in his city, in his house, there was nothing to stand between them but what they put there themselves.

Thorsten set two plates on the round metal table in the

center of the room. Next he carried in a platter filled with nuts, dried dates, raisins, and slivers of fresh ginger. Each time he entered the room Shannon felt the subtle current between them. She wondered when he would make a move, and what it might be.

"Do you need help?" she asked.

"No. Almost finished."

Shannon continued surveying his work. How could someone capture the world this way? She had never been able to take a decent photo—her thumb was featured in more pictures than she cared to admit. But this was more than taking a good picture. This was seeing something—the beauty in simple nature—and translating into art.

She stole a glance toward the kitchen, where Thorsten ladled creamy soup into two deep bowls. He pulled a loaf of bread from the oven and laid it in a basket. Shannon watched him carefully arrange bowls and the basket on a wicker tray, roll two cloth napkins and lay them along side, then select two spoons from a small collection of utensils sprouting from a drinking glass on the counter. She quickly turned back to the photos as he hefted the tray.

"I hope you like seafood."

"Love it."

She helped him unload the tray, and for the first time their hands touched. Without looking at him, she coiled her fingers around his and squeezed quickly before releasing. She sat down, still concentrating mightily on the food.

Thorsten poured two cups of tea. Ginger-scented steam rose from the cups. Shannon sipped, eyes closed, using the time to resteel herself. When she opened them again, Thorsten was watching.

"What?"

"I'm glad you're here."

She was sure she blushed. How could something so innocent sound so fraught with intent?

"Yeah, me, too," she answered a little too brusquely. *Down to business.* "So what's the plan for tomorrow?"

"The boat leaves at ten in the morning. I'll come get you at the hotel a little after nine."

*Good. He's not going to try to talk me into staying here.* "How long is the boat ride?"

"About five hours. It can be rough seas—is that a problem?"

"No." She patted her belly. "Cast iron."

She wasn't sure he understood, but he didn't ask again. Thorsten tore off a piece of warm, crusty bread and handed the basket to Shannon.

"I can't believe all this," she said. "Thank you."

"You're welcome."

She had been so absorbed in trying to appear unaffected, she hadn't had time to taste anything yet. She dipped her spoon into the soup and took her first exquisite bite. A gumbo, soft and smooth, lightly-spiced, warm and rich from the tiny shrimp and mussels at the top to the rice at the bottom.

"Oh, Thorsten..."

He smiled shyly. "You like it?"

Shannon set down her spoon and sat back. "Seriously, where did you learn to cook like this?"

"I was a chef for a few years—we passed the restaurant on our way here, but you probably didn't notice. And I like to cook, so I try new foods all the time."

"You know what Baby Michael would say right now."

"I'm more interested in what you will say." He gazed at her with a directness that made her toes curl.

Shannon nervously tucked her hair behind her ear and leaned back over the soup. "I say it's pretty great."

"You know what I mean," he pressed.

She lingered over another spoonful. *Now what, Shan? What happened to that talent for thinking on your feet?* "I think we'll see," she hedged. "But if you keep making me nervous like this, there's no way I'll be able to enjoy my meal. And I really want to enjoy it."

"Then here, try this." He selected a dried date and held it to her lips. "Take a bite, then drink some tea."

She let him feed her, knowing it was one more step in a direction she shouldn't go. Her lips skimmed his fingers. She was tempted to flick her tongue against them, to give up all resistance, to follow where her body was leading her and where Thorsten obviously wanted her to go.

Cradling the date in her mouth, she took a sip of steeped ginger tea. The combination of saltiness and sweetness and the sharp tang of ginger lit her taste buds like a firecracker. She swirled the flavors across her tongue.

*I could kiss you right now. I might kiss you...*

"I can't believe how beautiful all of these are," she said, sweeping her hand across the room. "Do you sell them?"

"Sometimes."

"Where? How?"

"My boss keeps a few in his office. Sometimes customers buy them."

"That's all? You haven't tried to do more?"

"No."

She had found something safe to talk about. "Thorsten, that's crazy. These pictures are really great. You could make a lot of money selling them. People love that stuff. You could make cards or calendars and sell prints—"

Thorsten shrugged.

"I'm serious. I'll bet every tourist who comes here wants pictures like this to take home. You could make a lot of money."

He shrugged again. "It's not that important. I don't take photos for the money."

"I know that, but listen to me." She felt in control again. This was something she could do—create a business plan. She did it all the time for clients. "You probably have a thousand pictures in here. You could sell every one of them to some calendar or greeting card company. Or you could print them yourself and sell them over the Internet. You could even put together a book of photos and sell them at the gift shops."

Thorsten wiped his mouth and leaned back in his chair. "And then what?"

"And then you keep doing it. Just keep taking pictures you want to take. People will want to buy them."

Thorsten interlaced his fingers across his stomach. He regarded her with sphinx-like ambiguity. "Why? So I can move to a better place?"

"No." She glanced around them. "I think this place is great. That's not what I'm talking about—"

"Or so I can buy a fancy car?"

"No, none of that. It's just that if you're doing this anyway, you should share it with people. And people will pay you for it. That's all I'm saying. You have a product, people will want it, so you should take advantage of that."

"I should."

"Yes. I can show you how if you want. I'm good at this stuff."

"Maybe later." His voice was dull, his expression unreadable. Had she said something wrong? Somehow the mood had shifted without her knowing. It was as though a fog had drifted into the room and blocked out what was left of the sun.

"I'm sorry," she tried. "Is this bothering you?"

He stood and lifted his bowl. "No, it's very interesting. Would you like more tea?"

Shannon downed the last few bites of gumbo and carried the rest of the dishes to the kitchen. Thorsten stood at the sink washing his bowl and spoon.

Shannon took a chance and rested her palm against his back.

Thorsten met her eyes. "Let me show you something," he said.

She followed him to the middle of three bedrooms. If the first bedroom had been his gallery, this was the library. Bookshelves covered every inch of wall space from floor to ceiling. A stack of books sat at the foot of the ratty green upholstered chair in the center of the room.

Shannon surveyed the selections: many foreign titles she took to be Icelandic, but just as many familiar English and American titles. Works by Hemingway, Thomas Hardy, Robert Frost, Robert Browning. Thoreau and T. H. White and Pat Conroy. Adventure travelogues by Tim Cahill and Jon Krakauer and various polar explorers.

"Who are you?" Shannon asked him. "I don't believe we've met."

"Why? You didn't think I could read?" he asked with a smile.

"I didn't think anyone could read this much. Unless it's all for show."

"No, I've read them all—or most of them. I still have some I need to get to this winter."

"So is this what you do all winter?"

"Yes, a lot of the time. I work in the shrimp factory—we passed it coming from the bus depot—and I ski and I read."

"Wow." She stared at him with renewed wonder. "This is really great. I think you have a pretty great life."

He smiled. "I think so, too."

He closed the distance between them so quickly she barely had time to consider whether she wanted that. Of course she wanted it, she thought. It was what she had wanted all night.

If he meant to kiss her in such a way she would forget her name, her nationality, where she was staying for the night—he was doing it. Shannon lost herself in the sensation: the taste of his mouth, the sound of his quickened breath, the feeling of his hands pulling her toward him, pressing her hips against his, testing the need in both of them.

"You should stay here," he murmured.

*I know. I absolutely know.*

"I can't," she answered. She didn't expect the catch in her voice. *Why not? Why can't you?* "I don't think it's a good idea."

"It's the best idea." His hands were warm against her bare back. His fingers lingered over the clasp of her bra. Then he released it with a single twist.

Shannon caught her breath. *Just go with it.* She guided his hand to her breast. After so long waiting for it, the sensation was richer than she expected. His hand was soft and warm and squeezed when she wanted pressure, stroked when she wanted less.

Shannon groaned and forced herself to step back. She stared at him with sleepy-eyed animal lust. "You have no idea how much I want this." She clasped both of his hands in hers and squeezed hard. "Thorsten, this is such a bad idea—you don't even know."

"Why?" There it was again, that low husky voice that had led to their night of silent exploration while camping with her brothers. "I think it's the best idea I've ever had."

The tear surprised her. It sneaked from one eye and slid down her cheek before she even realized it was there. She swiped it away with her finger. "I have to go. Maybe I shouldn't have come." She stepped blindly toward the doorway, searching for the quickest escape.

Thorsten caught her arm. "Shannon, stop this. Why do you keep running away?"

"Because this isn't what I want."

"Why? What do you want? I don't understand you."

The fingers of emotion strummed across her heart. It wasn't about lust or a challenge or any of that anymore, Shannon realized. The problem was and had been the same from the beginning: This was a man she could love. This man could be the one finally to prove her wrong. Maybe a lifetime with one person was possible. Maybe she had been given a second chance to make the right choice.

Doubt devoured her. *You thought Erik was the one—remember? Since when do you know what you're doing when it comes to love? Repeat the same mistake, expect the same result. Go ahead—fall in love with him. You know exactly how it will turn out.*

He pulled her toward him. "Shannon—"

She wrenched her arm free. "I have to go." She escaped down the hall, swept her coat from the hook, bounded down the stairs and out into the sunlit night.

THORSTEN SLUMPED into the doughy green chair.

He should go after her, he knew, but he didn't have the strength at the moment. His body thrummed with desire. Where had he gone wrong? When did he lose her? He replayed the night word by word, gesture by gesture. She had been so close to saying yes—he had seen it in her eyes, felt it in her touch. Why was she holding back? And more important, what could he do to convince her it was safe to give in?

No matter how much he wanted to indulge in this micro-analysis, the fact remained that Shannon was out there somewhere not knowing where she was going.

Thorsten had no doubt someone would offer directions if she asked, but his own duty was clear. He rose from the chair and followed her path of flight.

He watched from a distance as she made her way down the central street back in the direction from which they had come. If she kept on this path, she would reach the hotel. Still, he wanted to make sure.

She had slowed enough that he could catch her now, if he wanted to. Unconsciously, his pace quickened. When they were a block apart she turned and saw him. She waited for him to catch up. He met her on the corner in front of the grocery store.

Her cheeks were rosy, her gray-green eyes bright with emotion. "I'm sorry," she offered. "I shouldn't have left like that."

He was surprised to find her so complacent already. He had expected a sharper greeting.

"I wanted to make sure you found the hotel."

"I see it up there. Thanks." She jammed her hands into the pockets of her coat. She looked up at the sky, then back at him. "I'm a little confused."

Thorsten smiled with relief—they weren't so far apart after all. "It's all right."

"Do you still want to take me backpacking?"

"Yes."

Shannon nodded. "Okay. What time should I be ready?"

"Nine-fifteen. Make sure you have a big breakfast first—if you really don't get sea sick."

She wrapped her arms across her chest and considered him for a moment. Her eyes softened. She stepped closer.

Thorsten opened his coat and wrapped her inside, holding her close against his chest.

He could feel her relax against him. "Are you all right?"

Shannon nodded. "Just a little gun shy."

"Gun shy?"

She tipped her head back and rested her chin on his chest. "Nervous. Skittish."

Up the street Thorsten saw a familiar face. The woman caught his eye and continued purposefully toward them. He tensed slightly and wrapped Shannon tighter in his embrace. Shannon studied his face with curiosity, then turned to follow his gaze.

Of course she wouldn't keep walking—that wasn't Bjarta's way. She stopped beside them and regarded Shannon with open curiosity. "*Gott kvöld*," she greeted them both.

"Bjarta." Thorsten released Shannon from his embrace, but still clung to her hand. He asked in English, "How are you tonight?"

She answered in Icelandic and added a question of her own, purposefully cutting Shannon from the conversation. Shannon loosened her grip and seemed ready to widen the distance between them, but Thorsten squeezed her hand for reassurance. "Were you full tonight?" he asked in English.

"*Nei.*" Bjarta launched into another round of Icelandic, but Thorsten cut her off.

"English, please. Bjarta works at the hotel," he explained to Shannon.

Bjarta smiled grimly. "Yes." She cast an appraising eye over Shannon. "Are you staying there?"

"I am," Shannon responded. Thorsten noted the clarity

and confidence in her voice. There was that toughness she had shown him when they first met. She did not need his protection from Bjarta. "I've heard it's a very nice place."

Bjarta resorted to her native tongue. "What's wrong, Thorsten, couldn't get her into your bed? How sad for you." In English she told Shannon, "Yes. A very nice place."

Thorsten smiled blandly at his former lover. He resisted the urge to carry on a private conversation with her in which he might remind her of the many deficiencies in their short-lived relationship. Instead he said in English, "We have to go now. Have a good night."

Bjarta smiled grimly. In Icelandic: "And better luck with this one. I hate to think you should ever spend a night alone."

Thorsten walked away, still holding Shannon's hand. When they were out of earshot, Shannon asked, "Another conquest?"

"A friend."

"Am I a friend?"

"I hope so."

"Somehow, stud, I have the feeling you have lots of friends in this town."

"A few, but nothing to worry about."

She pulled her hand free and buried both hands in her pockets, but stayed close enough to brush her arm against his as they walked. "We all have a past, Thorsten."

"*Já.*"

"I won't ask about yours if you won't ask about mine."

If there was a right thing to say just then, he didn't know

what it was. Thorsten threaded his arm through hers and guided her the last few steps to the hotel.

Shannon halted in the lobby. "Luggage. I forgot my bag."

"I'll go get it."

"Do you mind?"

He leaned close and whispered, "What I mind is you staying here instead of with me."

"Sorry, that's the deal."

Thorsten's throat constricted. What were the right words? What could he say right now, right here, to convince her to turn around and come back with him? Why were they wasting all this time dancing around each other, when they should already be lovers, already be spending every night in each other's arms?

But it was more than that. He wanted to reach inside her heart and pull her to the surface and understand everything she was and felt and wanted. She was vulnerable in a way he couldn't classify, couldn't solve. She needed something from him, but maybe even she didn't know what it was. If so, what chance did he have of discovering it?

"Wait here," he told her. "I'll be right back."

He ducked back into the crisp air, still puzzling over how to turn the night around. What, he thought as he walked along, had he hoped would happen that night? Part of the answer was obvious: He wanted to make love to her, as often and as well as he could. He had thought earlier in the evening they were on an unstoppable course to his bed, but as usual Shannon had proven too disciplined. He admired her strong will, but he couldn't help wishing for less of it when his hands were on her bare skin and his hips were grinding against hers and their mouths were hungry for each other.

Beyond that, what had he wanted? For her to see him as he was—no pretense, no bravado, no exaggeration. She had seen some of what he was tonight, and from what he could tell, she seemed to like what she saw. He had brought enough women to his apartment to know how to gauge their response. Some were intrigued by his pastimes, others scornful of them, still others more focused on the squalid surroundings of the attic rooms to notice anything else.

Then there were women like Bjarta, who only craved a good romp in his bed, and had no desire to know anything more about him. At times that was certainly enough for him, too. But he wanted much more from Shannon.

He retrieved her luggage and hoisted her pack. He hadn't noticed before how heavy it was. Generally he liked his clients to carry only a third of their weight on backpacking trips—less, if possible. He set it back down and removed the nylon cover Shannon had cinched around the pack to protect it from the rain.

On the outside of the pack, beneath the thin bag holding her sleeping pad, lay the unmistakable bulk of a tent bag. He felt for the poles to be certain.

*Three steps forward, five steps back.* What had he expected? She wasn't sleeping with him now, so why would she magically come to him once they were outside?

He replaced the rain cover and shouldered the pack, then lifted her carry-on. All the way back to the hotel he considered what he should say about it. Nothing, was the answer.

He had nothing to gain by forcing her to continue pushing him away.

He dropped the pack and bag beside her chair. "Okay, see you tomorrow."

"Wait." She stood and walked him to the door. "Um, okay." She reached awkwardly for his hand. "Thanks for dinner."

He squeezed her warm fingers. "You're welcome. Get some sleep."

He pushed through the glass doors before he could be tempted to say anything else.

At least now he knew where he stood. He would know even more tomorrow if the tent were still strapped to her pack when she met him.

*"I won't ask about yours if you won't ask about mine."* What was it about her past that stood between them now? Why did she always pull away?

And what could he do to convince her that what was happening was right for both of them?

Six days— that was all he had to make her change her mind. And if he couldn't, what then? Just forget about her? Put her on the bus and wave goodbye and go back to living as he had?

Impossible. He had seen the other side. He could never pretend life might be as good without her. If he had never been certain of anything before, he was certain of this: There had always been a piece of his life missing, and Shannon held it in her hands. Wasn't it possible she felt the same way about him? Weren't they reflections of each other, each of them wanting the same things, each of them offering what the other needed?

Thorsten rounded the corner and spied Bjarta from a distance. She sat waiting on the steps outside his apartment. He slowed, cursing to himself. Just one more reason to appreciate Shannon, he thought. She would never do something like this.

Bjarta had changed into form-defining knit pants and taken her hair down. She smelled strongly of perfume. "Who's the girl?" she asked.

"Go home, Bjarta." He unlocked the door and slipped through without looking back.

Bjarta knocked, first lightly, then with more force. Thorsten paused on the stairs. He returned to the ground floor and opened the door.

Bjarta tipped her head coyly and trickled her finger down his chest. "Thorsten..."

He caught her finger and steered it away. "I'm not interested. Good night."

Bjarta's eyes narrowed. "No? Since when?" She stroked lower this time.

Thorsten diverted her hand and stepped back. "I'm serious, Bjarta. Go home." He closed the door on her pout and mounted the stairs. His groin throbbed involuntarily, but he knew Bjarta was not the cause. If he had to wait, he would wait. He wouldn't ruin his appetite on anything less than what he really wanted.

He lay awake reimagining the scene in the library. *"I think it's the best idea I've ever had,"* he tells her. This time she doesn't pull away. He undresses her slowly, deliberately torturing them both with delay. Frustrated, she takes matters into her own hands. Takes control. Takes what she wants...

Thorsten allowed the sensation to build, and resisted doing anything about it. It would make it that much sweeter when they both finally gave in.

*Six days, five nights. Nothing but time alone.*

Separate tents? He'd have to see about that.

## 10

He found Shannon waiting in front of the hotel the next morning. She wore her black hiking pants and her blue fleece coat. Her cheeks were rosy with cold. Thorsten wore a baseball cap and wind-resistant pants and an expedition-weight fleece shirt that had seen its share of weather.

She mentioned she had left her carry-on in the care of the hotel.

But not, Thorsten noted, her tent. There it was, still strapped to her pack.

*Fine,* he reassured himself. *A temporary situation.*

Shannon pulled on her rain coat.

"You brought rain pants, too?" Thorsten asked.

"Yes."

"How many pairs of long underwear?"

"Thorsten, I know how to pack."

"Not here. How many?"

"Two. The ones I'm wearing and another one."

"The most important thing is to always have one set of dry clothes, socks to underwear to shirt."

"I have it. I'll be fine."

Why was he harping on her this way? he wondered. Habit, he supposed, from having taken so many novices into the backcountry. And maybe a little anger, he admitted, over seeing the tent again.

They hiked the short distance to the dock, where they joined a group of passengers waiting to board the small ferry.

"Are all these people backpacking the same place we are?" Shannon asked.

"No. They're all going to Hornstrandir, but the boat stops at four or five fjords on the peninsula. Some people just go overnight and camp on the beach. The boat picks them up the next day."

"Does the captain already know where to pick us up at the end of our hike?"

"I know my job," Thorsten answered. He didn't mean it to sound as harsh as it did. He smiled softly to take away the sting. "Relax. I'll take care of you."

Shannon seemed to understand he was tired of joking with her. She nodded soberly. "I know you will."

He draped his arm lightly around her shoulder and gave her a light peck on the cheek. "I hope you like this place as much as I do. I want you to have a good time."

He was pleased to feel her lean against him instead of pulling away. "I will. Thanks for asking me."

They settled onto seats inside the cabin. While Shannon

studied the map, Thorsten studied the other passengers. There were twenty or so, most of them Icelanders. A German couple, two Swedes. No other Americans. No other guides—at least none that he recognized. The high season for backpacking the Hornstrandir peninsula didn't begin for another few weeks. Thorsten's boss usually sent him on a pre-season scouting trip to check the condition of their traditional routes, since a winter of snow and rain could obliterate what might have been a passable trail the year before. Thorsten had already been once that month, but convinced his boss a second trip would be ideal for scouting more trails. He had cajoled boat passage for Shannon as well. As the senior guide for the company's kayaking and backpacking excursions, Thorsten had earned a few privileges. Taking along a companion every now and then was one of them.

In the past he had used these trips as a crucible for his relationships—at times, if he cared to admit it, as an excuse to end them. If a romance seemed to be progressing too well or too quickly, he might test it with a week of cross-country skiing or cold water kayaking or backpacking on Hornstrandir. Hardships and a little discomfort tended to bring out a woman's true personality.

Those four days backpacking with Shannon in Arizona were the best Thorsten had ever had with a woman. If only they had slept together every night, the trip would have been perfect.

As the ferry drew closer to the first fjord, Thorsten joined some of the other passengers on deck. The wind and spray were bracing, and they infused him with an energy he could never find anywhere else. This place was in his veins. He loved its massive, overpowering cliffs, the swarms of sea birds, the clouds that cushioned the ridges, hiding them from the casual eye. Seamen swore they saw fairies here, and elves, and schools of mermaids. Storms swept their boats against the rocks and drove men to their underwater graves, but year after year for centuries they had continued coming, fishing Hornstrandir's fjords and mining her cliffs for precious eggs.

Shannon joined him on deck. Within minutes her teeth chattered, but her smile never faded. She leaned closer to him for warmth. Thorsten wrapped his arm around her. He pressed his mouth to her ear so she could hear above the din of waves and wind.

"Excited?"

She nodded.

"Ever seen anyplace like this?"

"Never."

"I wanted to show it to you. This is the best of Iceland."

When her shivers did not abate, he convinced her to go inside. "I'll come in a few minutes," he promised.

As the boat drew closer to shore inside the first fjord, Thorsten spied a flash of white far down the beach.

He squinted into the spray, trying to make out the scene.

Two hikers barreled across the sand waving a white T-shirt like a flag.

Thorsten tapped on the captain's window and pointed. The captain nodded and grinned. "Looks like they're surrendering," he shouted to Thorsten.

The couple continued to run, their backpacks pounding

against their backs, while the crew loaded gear into the inflatable outboard boat that would ferry passengers the rest of the way to shore. Six passengers and their assorted provisions made the first trip. The white-flag team continued to run, although their pace had slowed. On the second trip, four more passengers embarked with their gear. By then the runners had dropped down to a walk.

The inflatable's captain waited for them, then ferried them back to the boat. The couple collapsed onto seats inside the cabin. Their clothes, boots, hair—everything was soaked through.

"What happened?" Shannon asked them. Thorsten smiled. Only an American would be so forthright.

"Damn rain," the man answered in a British accent. He was mid-fifties, portly, but not as out of shape as Halldor or some of Thorsten's other clients over the years. The man's wife looked fitter, although it was hard to tell with her slumped in the seat, staring ahead in a stupor of exhaustion.

"Our tent floated two nights ago," the man continued. "Sleeping bags sopping, not a dry stitch of clothes—miserable. We spent the night in the emergency shelter. Didn't know if the boat was scheduled to come in today. Took us by surprise—you saw us running." He leaned back and closed his eyes. "Miserable place."

Shannon poked her elbow against Thorsten's side. "You poor things."

The wife answered in monotone, "Pizza and beer. It's all I've been promising myself for hours."

The man patted her leg. "You'll get it tonight, my dear."

The woman smoothed a hand over her wet hair. "Never seen it so bad."

"Lot of rain on Hornstrandir," one of the Icelandic passengers offered. "No surprise there."

The woman looked at him blankly. "But so much! The inside of my boots are ponds."

Her husband patted her leg again, then leaned back again, eyes closed, mouth open as though ready to snore.

Thorsten glanced at Shannon. She smiled and coaxed him closer. "Where have you brought me?" she whispered.

He tickled his lips against her ear. "To your doom," he whispered ominously. He kissed her cheek. To his delight, she turned her head and met his lips with hers. The kiss was light, friendly, quick. But it was something—a connection at a time when he wondered where to go next.

Another two hours, more passengers disembarking at another fjord, then the boat pulled into Hornvík. Mist hid the enormous wall of bird cliffs that loomed over the fjord. A light rain fell, but Thorsten could see pockets of blue sky in the distance.

Shannon had fallen asleep against his shoulder. Thorsten nudged her gently. "We're here."

The Brits had fallen asleep, too—the great, sloppy sleep of bodies pushed to their limit. Shannon glanced at the still-sodden couple.

"Pizza and beer, huh? Is that how I'll be at the end of this trip?"

"I can get you both. But first you have to earn it."

"Oh, really?" she asked dryly.

"By hiking," he clarified, although he didn't mind the

other interpretation, either. *I'll give you whatever you want,* he thought. *Pizza and beer are the least of it.*

The last of the passengers stood on deck waiting for their turn in the inflatable. Thorsten and Shannon went with the second group.

It was 3:30. Thorsten had planned to make a side trip up to the bird cliffs that afternoon, then camp in the established campground near the beach, but the weather suggested a better alternative. With the bird cliffs hidden in cloud and mist, and the rain falling so lightly, it made more sense to set out along the trail and put as much mileage behind them as possible before sharper weather set in.

"Does that sound all right?" Thorsten asked.

"Whatever you say."

He smiled mischievously. "Oh, really? Whatever I say?"

"Within reason."

"Too bad." He took a chance and added, "Are you sure you want to bring that tent? It's a lot of weight, and I brought one."

"I'm sure." She averted her eyes.

What was that? he wondered. Uncertainty? Second thoughts? He decided not to push her. They could ditch the tent anywhere along the way. They had hours before they would stop for the night.

They both donned rain gear, and secured the rain covers over their packs. As the other passengers headed for the campground, Thorsten and Shannon began their trek along the beach.

He glanced back at her every now and then, and always

found her looking out into the distance at the sea or the cliffs across the fjord.

"What do you think?" he finally asked.

"I think my brothers are going to love this."


*WHY ARE you thinking of them?* Shannon wondered. Ever since the boat neared that first fjord, her brothers had been on her mind.

She would bring them back here and show them what she found. She was the advance party. They would love it here.

And that made her think of the future. Already she knew she would come back. And what did that mean? Would she see Thorsten again? How could she avoid it? Why should she avoid it?

What a miserable night she had had. As the hours ticked by she wondered why she was there in that pleasant but empty room, sleeping alone on her side of two twin beds pushed together. Thorsten's bed would be warm. Thorsten's body...

Twice she rose from bed and began to dress. The sky was still light—she could find her way there easily.

*And then?*

*And then get over this ridiculous bout of chastity. Since when do we deny ourselves anything? Since when do we turn away the kind of thrills Thorsten is offering?*

Twice she pulled on her pajamas again and lay back down.

In the morning she ate without tasting, simply to get the

calories into her body. When he met her outside the hotel he seemed bright and perky, and she hated him for it. *No lost sleep there.*

The sway of the boat had fed her drowsiness. She meant to pay closer attention to the scenery, but she could barely focus. Then the retreating Brits had livened the afternoon, and filled her with renewed enthusiasm for what lay ahead. This place would be a challenge. No groomed trails like in the National Parks, no rescue teams waiting for a call from the cell phone—Hornstrandir was so remote, cell phones wouldn't work. Just her and Thorsten and their years of accumulated skill and knowledge. What better way to spend six days of her life?

Her brothers would love this, yes, but she wanted to think of herself first.

As she hiked along the narrow trail leading from shore to an inland route, Shannon considered where she had gone wrong in her life. Here she was, thousands of miles from work and home, as content as she had ever been. The world felt clean and wide open, ready to hand her everything she asked for.

Including love.

The ache in her body radiated from her heart. She knew what she wanted, but she wasn't giving to herself, and that was worse than any physical pain she had ever endured.

What was wrong with falling in love? It had its benefits: that giddy sense of contentment, shiny hair, strong teeth—everything good. There he was, right in front of her, as available as any man could be.

"Thorsten?"

He turned and she lost the words.

*What now? Tell him it's all been a big mistake—that you meant to go through with it last night, that you're tired of waiting and putting him off and dying a little every time you see him?*

"Uh, can you just stop a minute?"

*Tell him! Don't be such a chicken.*

"It's really beautiful here."

He gazed out toward the ocean. "It's even better when the sky is clear. Maybe tonight some of this will blow off and you can see the cliffs."

Shannon nodded. Her palms sweated. *Say something, you miserable weakling.*

"Up ahead," Thorsten said pointing, "there's a rope ladder, then we go further in, away from shore. I thought we would take a break in about an hour and have some soup. Then keep hiking as long as the weather is good—"

"Sure, sure, that sounds good."

The moment was gone. She felt it leave like a rush of cold air against her neck. She lowered her head and took a few steps forward. Thorsten turned and continued up the trail.

True to his word, an hour later they sat with their backs to the wind while Thorsten fired up the micro stove and boiled a pot of water.

The scent of bubbling soup lured a shy visitor. It was like a scene from a cartoon: the ribbon of steam flowing from the pot, straight to the nose of a brown Arctic fox. He loped toward them, bold at a distance, more cautious the closer he came. Soon he was within reach. Shannon stared in silent fascination.

Even the slightest movement from either her or Thorsten sent the creature scurrying back, but the scent continued to pull him in like a tractor beam.

"That's the only animal you'll see out here," Thorsten said. "No bears, no deer—"

"I thought you had reindeer in Iceland. Didn't I see a picture of that somewhere?"

"Not here. A few places on the island, but not on Hornstrandir."

She accepted a bowl of vegetable and pasta soup. Rain had been sputtering since they sat down, but now it was too heavy to ignore. She pulled up the hood on her coat and huddled over the soup bowl.

"How do you feel?" Thorsten asked her.

"Good. Fine."

He studied the sky. "The rain won't last—look at all the blue over there. If the weather is good, I'd like to hike until about ten o'clock. Is that all right?"

"Sure. Will it get dark at all tonight?"

"For an hour or so early in the morning."

A blast of wind rattled the screen around the stove. Thorsten scooted closer to Shannon. "Cold?"

"A little." She leaned against him and felt the immediate infusion of heat. "That's better."

He wrapped his arm across her waist and slipped his hand into her coat pocket. "Can I tell you something?"

*Warning.* "Yes."

"I've been thinking about this day since I first met you in April."

"You saw me at the rehearsal dinner and thought, 'I'm taking her to Hornstrandir'?"

"Yes. Exactly."

Shannon turned her head just enough to feel his breath against her cheek. So close, so intimate, so comfortable...

She felt unreasonably shy, as skittish as the fox. "Why?"

"I don't know why," Thorsten answered. "I thought you might like it here."

"I do like it here. It's beautiful."

"Do you like it here with me?"

"Yes."

"Are you happy you came?"

"Yes." *Tell him now—it's perfect.* "We should probably go. The rain—"

"In a minute." He tilted her face toward his and brushed his lips against hers. Electricity pumped through her veins. Warmth spread through her torso.

Rain pattered their hoods and streamed down their faces as they lost themselves in the kiss. Thorsten leaned back against the heath and pulled Shannon with him. He rolled her onto her back and positioned himself to shield her from the rain. He cradled her face in his hands and kissed her tenderly on the cheeks, the lips, the eyes, then returned for a more insistent taste of her mouth.

They could pitch a tent right there, Shannon thought. Go inside and wait out the rain. Spend all night exploring each other.

They could spend their time not just witnessing the spectacle of nature, but experiencing the wonder of their own undeniable attraction and the attachment that had grown steadily over the months they were apart, and seemed to have reached full force now that they were together again.

They could do all that and still make the boat in six days. Time was irrelevant. What mattered now was discovering what they had to offer each other.

"We should go," Shannon repeated.

"Not yet."

Thorsten's cold hand maneuvered beneath her coat. Rain dripped from the hem onto her bare belly. She shivered.

"Shannon, I've never wanted a woman so much."

And that's when, inexplicably, she began to cry.

She tried to turn her face away—to hide the ugliness of it, the truth of it—but Thorsten wouldn't let her.

"Why are you crying? Tell me."

She shook her head and pushed him off. Thorsten sat up and waited.

Shannon stood. She walked a few feet away and stared out into the ocean.

And wondered desperately what had just happened.

## 11

He waited ten minutes before speaking. "We should go."

She nodded, her back still to him. The rain and wind were both coming harder, and Thorsten worried their bodies would cool too much if they didn't keep moving.

She wouldn't meet his eye. Fine. She needed time. Fine.

But he would be damned if he let this go on much longer.

He loved her. He was tired of pretending it wasn't right to say that. He was tired of letting her get away with keeping him from saying it. If she didn't feel the same way, he wanted to know. If she did, he wanted to know that, too. As soon as possible.

He thought he understood her a little better now. Her armor had finally cracked. She didn't like it—that was clear, but it was also too damn bad. She would have to learn to live with having her heart displayed for him to see. If they were going to build any kind of life together—and that was where he hoped all of this was heading—she had to lay it all open for him now. He didn't want the dressed up, toughened up version of Shannon. He wanted what he saw when he watched her with her brothers and her cousin. He wanted that Shannon—the one who loved with all her heart. He didn't want one more day of this flimsy imitation. He wouldn't stand for it.

They hiked in silence for several more hours. Thorsten was afraid to say anything just yet, for fear it would come out angry. He was angry. They had wasted so much time. There was no excuse for it.

At 10:00 the sky was still light, but any hint of blue sky was gone. An ever-increasing wind slapped the rain against their faces. It was time to rest for the night.

Thorsten searched for a flat, relatively dry campsite—always a challenge on the spongy heath. "This looks good," he said. "We'll stop here."

Shannon glanced at him sheepishly. Probably still embarrassed over her tears, he thought.

"Get over it," he muttered. He hadn't intended to say it out loud. He certainly hadn't meant it to sound so gruff.

"What?"

"Nothing." He unpacked his tent and began erecting it. Shannon did the same with her own.

"Why are you doing that?" he demanded.

Her voice was weak. "Because. I think it would be better."

"How would it be better?"

"Thorsten—" Her face dissolved into tears again. She turned and continued her task.

*Take a deep breath,* Thorsten coached himself. This wasn't how he wanted it.

"Shannon," he tried again, "it makes more sense to share a tent. It will be warmer. The weather tonight—"

"I know," she conceded, her voice stronger now. "Just let me do it."

Dinner was a somber affair. Thorsten cooked with a minimum of frills—no fancy extras like the last time they backpacked together. He could have done more—he had the supplies—but his heart wasn't in it.

"Thank you," she said when she finished her meal. "I'm tired. I'm going to bed." She took a few steps toward her tent, then turned. "I'm sorry, Thorsten. I don't know what's wrong with me—I really don't. I'm very sorry. I promise I'll be better in the morning." A gust of wind slashed through the campsite. Shannon buried her hands in the pockets of her coat. "And I'm truly grateful you brought me here. I can't believe how beautiful it is."

She disappeared inside her tent, leaving Thorsten to puzzle over the day.

One thing was certain: He wasn't leaving Hornstrandir until he heard the truth.

THE DAY'S emotion weighed her down more than the physical effort. Shannon fell asleep almost immediately.

She awoke at 2:00 AM to the sound of wind battering her tent. It snapped against the fabric, whipping it so loudly she thought at any moment the next sound would be of the tent ripping apart. The poles shuddered violently. This wasn't the sturdy four-season tent she and Annie had slept in at Breidafjördur Bay—this was a simple three-season tent that until this moment she had always trusted to protect her from the elements. But now it seemed as flimsy as rice paper.

She lay in anxious hyperawareness for the next half hour. Rain assaulted the tent in waves, as though someone were tossing bucket after bucket of water on top of her. She considered calling out to Thorsten—for what? Reassurance? Help? Hers was the last voice he wanted to hear right now, after the way she had treated him, going psycho on him like that. What must he think? Her tears after dinner flowed from embarrassment more than anything else. She was pathetic, and he had seen it.

A giant gust of wind heaved against the tent and finally succeeded in breaking it apart. A tent pole snapped. Fabric ripped open. Soon water and wind wailed into the tent, soaking everything inside.

"Thorsten! Thorsten!"

She quickly shoved what she could into her pack—shirt, socks, her boots. Her sleeping bag was already drenched. Frantically she salvaged what she could, knowing that every wet item she added to her pack only soaked what might have been dry inside it.

Where was he? Shannon unzipped the door, hoping to save the tent from ripping any more. She pulled her pack out, then her sleeping bag and pad.

"What are you doing?" Thorsten shouted. He had taken the time to dress in full rain gear. "You'll freeze out here! It's dangerous!"

Her sopping long underwear clung to her skin. Wind sucked the heat from her core. She knelt in a pool of frigid rainwater trying to stuff her sleeping bag into her pack.

"Shannon!" He gripped her by the shoulders and pulled her to her feet. "Look at me! Get inside! Take everything off. You'll freeze to death." He pushed her toward his tent. He bent to unzip the door. "Take it all off before you get inside. Don't get anything wet. Understand?"

Her teeth chattered. She didn't move, but simply stared.

"Shannon! Understand?"

Thorsten pulled her shirt over her head. "Take off your pants! Hurry!" When she still didn't budge, he did it for her. Then he removed her socks. "Get inside!" He pushed her through the tent door, then reached inside for his fleece coat. "Dry yourself off with this, then get in my bag."

Her body shook uncontrollably. She couldn't follow his instructions. A part of her brain knew she was already hypothermic, but she couldn't force herself to react. All she could do was stare.

Thorsten quickly wiped her down and dried her hair as best he could, then helped her into the sleeping bag.

"My pack—" she chattered, "—my tent—"

"I'll get them. First you."

He zipped her into the bag and cinched the hood around her face. Her body continued to shake. Thorsten piled clothes on top of her and laid his backpack over her feet.

"I'll be right back," he said. "Let me see what I can save."

He zipped the tent closed. Shannon lost track of time. He might have been gone one minute or ten. All she knew was the cold.

He returned with her pack and a few loose items. He laid them inside the vestibule, then crouched to remove his rain gear. He carefully peeled off his clothes, leaving the wet layers outside in the vestibule. He entered the tent wearing only a long underwear top and bottom.

He unzipped the sleeping bag and slipped in next to Shannon. He draped himself over her and did his best to close the sleeping bag again.

The transfer of body heat had an immediate, profound effect. Shannon curled against him like a second skin. She sucked up his warmth like a drowning woman desperate for air. He was warm. He was there. She was all right.

When she awoke they still lay in a tight embrace. He had not let her go.

She stared into his face, the ragged stubble, the soft lines around his eyes and mouth. She studied his lips, parted slightly, a quiet steady breath moving through them. She lifted her hand and traced the top of his ear, then the line of his eyebrow, the curve of his temple. His eyes were open now. She had one more thing to do.

Shannon wrapped her arms around him and pulled him into her heart and began what she should have done so many times before. She kissed down the length of his throat, then pulled up his shirt and continued to map out a line.

She warmed her hands underneath his back before reaching under the rest of his clothes. She helped pull them off, then draped them over whatever bare skin the sleeping bag couldn't cover.

Rain hammered the tent, drowning out every sound but the ones from within.

They were warm now. Hands explored freely, mouths sucked and nipped. Tongue and lips caressing, tasting. His skin was smooth, salty. Muscles tensed and released as she roamed the geography of his form.

She wasn't afraid of it anymore—of showing him everything she was and everything she felt for him. They were too far beyond it now for her ever to pretend she wanted less than all of him, right now, right here.

She prolonged her anticipation to the point of pain, then finally took him in. And in that moment of perfect fusion she felt the tears come again and this time she let them wash her clean while she made love to a man she knew she honestly loved.

She felt made of one skin, his on hers, his body filling where she was empty, hers covering the grooves and swales where his muscle gave way to flesh. She ate hungrily at his plate, devouring every lust he had to offer her, every slow devoted breath, every sigh of love that moved from his lips to hers and back again.

He pulled her hips in closer and dove in deeper and they moved together with the elemental simplicity of waves against the shore and wind conjoining with the rain. They were slick with passion and thirsty for the climax but neither wanted it to end.

Thorsten shifted beneath her, pulling her on top without a break in the rhythm. Shannon pushed onto her hands, wanting the space to look at him, to run her fingers over his chest, to bend and tickle her tongue over his skin.

Thorsten groaned and pulled her to him. He clung to her tightly, just as he had when her body shook with cold. He matched her pace and carried her to the finish until they both cried out in exquisite agony.

They collapsed in a tangle of spent love. Soon the cold air chilled the sweat on their skin. Thorsten covered them with the sleeping bag and every warm piece of clothing he could find. Then they slept hard and fast, neither stirring until sun nudged their tent at midday.

Then they awoke and began again.

And this time Shannon said what she meant and heard what she needed to hear.

They were in love. It was settled. There was nothing more to discuss.

Not now, anyway. Not for as long as she could manage.

It was too pure. Too precious. Too fragile, she was afraid.

*I'll think about that tomorrow.*

She kissed her way back into oblivion.

12

"Admit I was right," said Thorsten.

"Ha! Never."

They surveyed the wreckage of her tent. Ribbons of fabric fluttered in the breeze. Her poles lay bent at artistic angles. Random items of clothing and gear lay sodden all around.

Thorsten slipped his arm around Shannon's waist and pulled her gently against his hip. "Admit I know more than you do about how to survive in Iceland."

"I'd like to see you handle the Rockies," Shannon countered. "Or the Windies, or the Grand Canyon—"

"I'd like to see that, too," Thorsten said. "Maybe someone will show me."

Shannon hesitated. "Maybe."

Thorsten studied her face. "We're not going to have a problem, are we?"

She laughed nervously. "What do you mean?"

"I worked very hard to make you tell me you love me—"

"You call that hard work?" she teased.

"—and I'm not going to forget you said it."

Shannon kissed his cheek. "I won't forget it, either. It's true." She bent to retrieve a sock. "All true."

"Then do you want to talk about the future?"

"Not especially."

"Why?"

She stopped gathering loose clothing and looked at him. "All right, let's hear your plan."

"My plan? I don't have one. I thought we should make one together."

"Can I tell you what isn't a plan?" Shannon asked. "Me turning into Annie. I'll admit I have the same problem she does with crying when we're in love, but I'm not her. I can't drop everything and move here and turn into an Icelander."

"All right. Fair."

"So that's why I decided not to think about it." She was surprised at the stridency in her voice. "I suggest you don't, either."

"Is that a command?"

"No, just a suggestion."

Thorsten sighed. She couldn't tell if he was irritated or merely frustrated. He worked in silence deconstructing her tent. He shoved the pieces into her pack and said, "I want to marry you."

"I'm sure you do."

"Why are you acting like this?" Thorsten demanded. "I thought we could stop this finally and be honest."

She stared at him with a mixture of defiance and fear. "Honest. Okay, honest. We hardly know each other."

"I love you."

"I think you do, Thorsten." Her voice was softer now, and she strived to keep it that way. "And I think I love you, too. I believe I do. But that's not the end of it. That doesn't suddenly solve everything."

"No, it's not the end—it's the beginning. We go from here and decide how to be together."

"And how do you think that will work out?"

He groaned, but also smiled as he gripped her by the shoulders. "I don't know. That's why I'm talking to you. I want to decide together."

A case meeting. Every Monday morning the attorneys in her firm gathered to discuss what new matters had come on board during the week past, and to hash out problems with existing cases. It was a brainstorming session, no idea too crazy to express, both sides of a case analyzed for potential weaknesses.

Shannon loved those meetings. She loved the give and take of them, the chance to fire up her brain and let it work on someone else's problem. It was always easier to see solutions when the case wasn't her own.

"We have two people," Shannon began, hoping Thorsten could adapt to the spirit of the game. "Compatible in many ways. The sex is great, she loves his cooking, he loves…"

"Her."

"Hm, I was looking for more, but okay, we can keep it simple. He loves her, and, I'll fully admit, she is seriously in love with him."

Thorsten smiled. "Thank you."

"But here's where we run into trouble—"

"Only if you let it," Thorsten answered softly. "Shannon, come here."

*You're not playing it right*, Shannon thought. *You're not supposed to look at me like that.* She sat down beside him. His lips were warm, the rest of his face cold.

"I don't want to talk about it like this," Thorsten said. "It's too important."

Her eyes met his. "I agree. It's too important."

"What do you want to do?" He wrapped his arm around her shoulders and let her soften against his side.

"I want to be in love for a few days and not worry about what happens after that."

"Do you want to be with me?" Thorsten asked.

"I do."

"For longer than a few days?"

"Yes. But I don't know how to make that happen, and I don't want to worry about it right now. Can you understand that? I just want this oasis of time here. I want to love you and be loved by you. Can't we think about the rest later?"

Thorsten sighed. He rested his chin on top of her head. "Shannon, I'm serious—I want to marry you."

"I've been married."

"I know. Your brothers told me."

"It's not so easy."

"Do you believe I love you?"

"Yes," she answered truthfully.

"Okay. That's all I need to know right now."

She tilted her face to look up at him. "Then we won't talk about it anymore? At least while we're here?"

"If that's what you want."

"I'd like to relax and enjoy you—completely. I don't want to worry about being sad while I do it."

"Okay." He kissed her hair. He stood and offered his hand. "Come on. We need to break camp and get to the shelter so we can dry your gear. We need your sleeping bag—mine isn't big enough alone."

Shannon wrapped her arms around his neck and kissed him. "Thank you, Thorsten. I love you."

He patted her rump. "Let's go. I want to show you more."


THEY WERE MARRIED on Christmas Eve.

Shannon and Erik waited in line at the courthouse with a few dozen other couples, young and old, all eager to begin their married lives by Christmas Day.

They wore their ski clothes so they could go directly from the courthouse to a nearby lake and cross-country ski around it, Erik in his rented top hat, Shannon in her veil. It was designed to be one more crazy event in what they promised would be a lifetime of crazy moments together.

Erik was a charmer, just like Thorsten. He was tall and blond and athletic, intelligent and socially adept. He had an easy sexuality about him, a way of making every woman in the room feel she could go home with him if she wanted. He wasn't crass about it—no innuendo or sophomoric come-ons. Instead he simply worked a crowd, giving full-body embraces that never lingered too long, touching often but not inappropriately, generally giving off the aura of untamed heat just waiting to explode.

They met in a philosophy class. Both were in their last semester of undergrad. Erik was going on to a Master's in Philosophy, Shannon planned to start law school in the fall.

She liked that he chose her. She didn't give in too easily, but it was in her mind from the moment they met. When she finally brought him to bed it was clear his experience had taught him much. While other men her age were still clumsily working out the mechanics of pleasing their women—while pretending that was more important to them than their own satisfaction—Erik had obviously paid attention to the finer points of seduction and consummation, and knew just what to do to turn a woman inside out.

He proposed one night after a particularly spirited session of lovemaking.

"Maybe we should get married someday."

"All right."

It was Thanksgiving weekend. They had been dating for six months.

Shannon treated the proposal more casually than she meant it. Erik was exactly what she wanted in a man—witty, charming, good-looking, and possessing a spirit of adventure to match her own. They had traveled around the country that summer, living out of her car and their backpacks. He skied, biked, hiked, did everything she loved to do. Even her brothers seemed to like him, although both Will and Chris hinted they had caught him being less than chaste on a road trip they had taken with him.

Shannon shrugged it off. "Women like him."

"He likes them," Chris pointed out.

"I'm sure he didn't do anything."

"Okay," her brother said. "Just wanted you to know."

Shannon could admit now, in retrospect, she worried about Erik's fidelity from the beginning. She wanted to take him off the market—as if pulling out all a shark's teeth could keep it from biting. Another set always grew back.

After the wedding they lived together in a guest house with rent small enough they could manage it with their combined wages as wait staff. Shannon attended law school during the day and worked nights and weekends at a German restaurant. Erik had decided to delay grad school for a year while he sorted through his future career options. He tended bar at a hangout near the university. It was meant to be temporary work while he searched for daytime employment, but the months coasted by and the tips were always too good and "Why shouldn't I work at night? You're never home anyway."

"Yeah, but I'd like to be," Shannon had answered. "This summer I want to get a clerking job at one of the law firms. I'm quitting the restaurant."

"All right," Erik agreed, "I'll quit then, too."

By July Shannon was leaving for work every morning dressed in high heels and a suit, while Erik slept off the effects of his late nights. He left for work at 4:00 in the afternoon and returned home after Shannon was already asleep. On the weekends she spent most of the time in the law library while Erik played basketball with his friends or went on hikes or rode his bike.

"It'll change soon," he claimed. "I just haven't found the

right job. And the money's good right now—it doesn't make much sense to quit."

In August Shannon began her second year of law school. That was about the same time, as best she could reconstruct, that Erik began his affair—at least the first one that she knew about for sure. Knowing him, there had been others.

Was it inertia that kept her from doing anything about it sooner? Or was it pride? A part of her wanted to pretend she didn't know what he was doing. They rarely made love anymore, and when they did it was hurried and aggressive and left her feeling raw with humiliation. No one would fix this but her. Erik obviously had no intention of leaving on his own.

He returned to the house early one morning to discover all traces of Shannon had been removed. She had waited until he left for work the day before, then with the help a few buddies from law school had rapidly packed everything in the house that belonged to her. Through a combination of her friend's ancient station wagon and her own two-door compact, they made several trips and hauled everything away before Erik returned home. She had even taken care of changing the utilities out of her name—an efficient mind at work.

She lived three months in a studio apartment near the law school. Her possessions stayed packed in boxes, stacked along the walls. She didn't want to make a home. She didn't know how to begin again.

Then Annie arrived. She flew up on her winter break from teaching and took one look at Shannon's apartment. "Oh, honey, no. This won't do."

Annie spent two days searching the paper for rentals, then forcing Shannon to go look at the prospects.

An old yellow house finally cured her. She stepped inside from the wrap-around porch and gazed about the small, one-bedroom house. Freshly-painted white panel walls, high ceilings, plenty of windows, a claw-foot tub in the tiny bathroom, a shady back yard perfect for summer reading—here was a place where she could begin again and create a life all her own. The house sat in downtown Minneapolis, in a section on its way to revitalization. Shannon felt the same way herself.

Annie helped Shannon unpack her boxes one by one, insisting that they not leave a single item hidden away. "If it doesn't fit, throw it away," Annie counseled. "You're staying here a long time."

By the end of Annie's vacation the house was home. Shannon's books filled the floor-to-ceiling bookshelves. Her pots hung from hooks above the stove. Her love-worn sofa had found a better home with the Salvation Army, and a clean new futon couch filled the space. Fresh daisies on her kitchen table, all her favorite photographs and prints on the walls—it was a joy to walk in every day and see such comfort waiting for her.

"Promise me you won't do this again," Annie told her.

"What—marry a loser?" A forbidden tear moistened Shannon's eye. The hurt still found ways of stinging her at unexpected times.

"No," Annie concluded, "don't give up on your life. You're far too amazing for that."

Shannon hadn't given up, but she had learned caution.

And the lessons Erik left her with had been too hard-won to forget, no matter how appealing Thorsten's offer was.

Fast love was bad love. It never lasted. *Repeat after me.*


THEY CAME over the pass and down a steep hill into the fjord. The orange emergency hut squatted on shore, smoke rising from its chimney.

"Looks like someone beat us to it," Shannon said.

"We won't stay the night."

A cluster of tents sat just outside the shelter. Shannon counted eleven. She could see people moving in and out of the shelter, but wasn't sure how many there were. A few of them stopped whatever they were doing to observe Shannon and Thorsten descend the hill. By the time the two reached the shelter, no one was outside. She entered the hut not knowing what to expect.

There were about twenty of them crammed inside the one-room shelter Clothing and sleeping bags hung from two makeshift clotheslines strung wall to wall. Heat radiated from the wood-burning stove. The room was humid with evaporation.

"*Góðan dag,*" Thorsten greeted the party.

"Hello," Shannon said.

The group of Icelanders looked from Thorsten to Shannon and settled on a menu of English.

"Good hiking?" a fit-looking, gray-bearded gentleman in his mid-60's asked.

"Yes," Thorsten answered. "Beautiful day."

"Where are you from?"

"Ísafjördur."

"And you?" the man asked.

"America," Shannon answered. She felt the spotlight shift.

Their host asked Thorsten a question in Icelandic. Thorsten answered in kind and winked at Shannon.

"What?" she asked.

Thorsten smiled and whispered, "I'll tell you later."

Their hosts offered hot water from the hot plate and a place to sit down. While Shannon squeezed onto an already-laden bench, Thorsten dug in his pack for two packets of cocoa.

Polite questions came flooding at Shannon from various members of the group: Where in America? What did she do there? Was this her first time in Iceland? How long was she staying? What did she think—did she like it?

She answered with genuine enthusiasm for the place and its people. When asked for details about their backpacking route, she gave as accurate an account as she could before appealing to Thorsten for help.

He rattled off place names and features with a melodic blend of Icelandic and English. More questions were directed at him, all in Icelandic.

Realizing she had nothing to contribute at the moment, Shannon tuned out the conversation. She let her eyes wander around the shelter, from the flat, stained mattress where several people reclined, to the shelves cluttered with mismatched cookware and dusty canned foods, to the wet sleeping bags and clothes hanging above their heads.

Soon Thorsten explained the wet gear. "They slept in their tents last night, but the storm flooded them."

"My bag actually floated," the older gentleman said. "It was a hard night."

Shannon nodded sympathetically. *At least mine ended happily.*

The group of Icelanders had pressed on to the emergency shelter first thing that morning, and now, hours later, they still waited for their gear to dry.

"We'll probably spend the night," the leader said. "Maybe tomorrow night, too. But it's all right—we still have five more days. The weather will improve by then!"

A middle-aged woman standing near Shannon shyly handed her a book. "You should write in this, if you want," the woman said. "Not many Americans come here."

Shannon flipped through the stiff pages. It was a log, a diary for seamen and hikers cataloging their reasons for seeking shelter in the hut over the years. Many entries were in Icelandic, but a few were in English.

"Threw one boot across the river," one hiker wrote. "Other one missed."

Shannon added her own few lines, expressing admiration for Hornstrandir's stark beauty and describing her tent's misfortune. She was just closing the book when she thought to add one more line.

She replaced the book on the shelf before Thorsten could see. She smiled inwardly, curious over her own contradictory behavior.

They sipped cocoa from their mugs and socialized a half hour or so, then bid the group farewell.

"So we won't try to dry anything here?" Shannon asked.

"No room," Thorsten answered. "We'll think of something else."

"So what did you say?" Shannon asked as soon as they were clear of the group. "To that man?"

"He wanted to know if you were *þessi elska*—my sweetheart."

"What did you tell him?"

"What do you think?"

Shannon considered telling him what she had written in the emergency log, but decided against it—he might misunderstand after everything she had said that morning. She linked her arm in Thorsten's and matched his longer stride.

"I'm ready to go back to bed," she murmured.

"Not until I dry your bag."

"We can share," Shannon argued.

"There's another hut at the next fjord. If it's empty we can spend the night."

"And if it's not?"

"Then we'll think of something else."

"Is that your answer to everything today?"

"I thought you didn't want to talk about the future. But yes, it is my answer to everything."

Shannon glanced at her lover's sober expression. Despite her misgivings, she wanted to know. "So that's your answer for me, too—about us? That you'll think of something?"

He kissed her cheek. "It's a long way to the next shelter. Let's try to reach it tonight."

## 13

Thorsten appreciated women. He had been pursuing them and catching them often enough since he was fifteen. Nearly twenty years of exploring what pleasures the feminine form had to offer. Like experimenting with foods, he enjoyed testing what tastes suited his palate, what colors and textures appealed to his senses, whether he liked something hot or cold, before dinner or after.

He brought that same inquisitive quality to his lovemaking with Shannon, and discovered there was nothing he wanted more than to prolong his time inside, to focus on her gray-green eyes, to try to read there what she was feeling and how he might draw it out of her and what he needed to do to keep her from retreating. She could seem so open and vulnerable to his love at one moment, and in the next return to that guarded position of loving and wanting him, but never too much.

He continued to coax the words from her, hoping that

the more she heard herself say she loved him, the more comfortable she would be with the truth of it. For she did love him—he had no doubt of that. Whatever burdens weighed on her heart, he knew in time he could chip away at them, and free her to love him as he loved her.

The gray-bearded man in the emergency shelter had asked more than Thorsten revealed. He wanted to know if Thorsten and Shannon were married.

"Not yet," Thorsten had answered, winking at Shannon.

He brought all his mind to bear on the problem. It was like solving a climbing route: studying the terrain, analyzing where the best line was, planting his ice ax in the right spot, testing his footing and his safety before taking the next step.

When they hadn't reached the second shelter by 11:00, Thorsten searched for a campsite and set up his tent. Shannon's sleeping bag was no less wet than that morning, so he decided they would have to make do with extra clothes draped over them and his compact emergency blanket close at hand. Rain fell again, but without the ferocious winds of the night before. Thorsten cooked Shannon a dinner of smoked sausage and creamy pasta with chunks of Parmesan cheese, followed by a dessert of hot chocolate and the coconut cookies she enjoyed on their kayaking trip. Then they undressed in the pale evening light and returned to where they had left their appetites that morning.

Thorsten knew better than to equate great sex with love. He had learned the distinction long ago. But loving a woman enhanced every physical pleasure, from the sight of her waking up naked beside him, to the sound of her voice, to the scent of her body after a night of passion. He had loved a few women in his life—his former girlfriend Gudrún, for one. He had also bedded many others without any pretensions toward love. Thorsten tried to separate what his body wanted from what his heart craved. Shannon, like a few other women, satisfied both desires. But unlike other women, Shannon had tapped into a deeper root—one Thorsten had never dared show anyone, for fear it would leave him with nothing.

What he wanted was family. Not simply children—although he would take as many of those as heaven allowed—but a feeling, a security, a collection of people connected by blood and history and affection and whatever else Shannon and her brothers and cousin seemed to have.

Thorsten had missed all that. His parents died a year apart when he was in elementary school. Kjartan was a few years older, and did his stoic best to shepherd his brother through the maze of foster care, but somehow the two never found the connection Thorsten saw in other brothers. Kjartan seemed to view his younger brother as his duty, rather than his companion. While their relationship now was friendly, it wasn't as close as Thorsten wanted. Kjartan didn't seem to want more, and Thorsten didn't force it. The love was either there or it wasn't. Like with Shannon and her brothers.

Seeing them together—at the wedding, on the backpacking trip, simply hanging around each other in easy, random moments—Thorsten felt that special ache reserved for the pains first planted in childhood. He imagined this was what it was like for women who couldn't bear children, seeing another woman round with the bounty of her own.

He could ignore the pain most of the time, but then he would catch a glimpse of a family out for picnic or father and daughter fishing together or a couple pushing a baby stroller, and the ache came throbbing back. He felt it on the kayaking trip watching Shannon bend her head toward Annie and share some private thought. He felt it when Shannon's brothers teased her and she gave it back with humor and a few jabs of her own. That was a family that liked each other, that loved each other. Any one of them could go away for a time, knowing they could always return and warm themselves by the flame of their family's love.

It was that love that Thorsten wanted to see in Shannon's eyes. He wanted to be her family. He wanted to know that who he was, right now, was enough for her, and that she loved him with the same faith she offered her family, that they would all manage life together never forsaking one another. That was the kind of love Thorsten offered her, whether she understood it or not. He wanted to tie himself to her life and weather whatever might come, joy or sorrow, feast or famine. He wanted to give her all the love in his heart and not see her turn away from it. And he wanted to create a family of their own together, to build on the foundation hers had laid.

He made love to her with his body while his heart pounded at her door. *Let me in, Shannon, let me in.* His own door was wide open, his heart vulnerable to the slightest nick, but he knew it was time to try. He had waited too long.


"YOU SHOULD THINK about what I said."

Thorsten knelt at the edge of a stream and trained his lens on a waterfall in the distance. "About what?"

"You could really do something with your pictures."

He glanced at her. "I already am."

"I mean you could do more."

Thorsten readjusted the settings on his camera, searching for the right mix of light. It was the first sunny day they had seen on Hornstrandir in four days, and he wanted to take advantage. The clouds had burned away, revealing blue sky and yellow light.

"If you want, I can help you," Shannon said.

Thorsten lowered his camera and sat back on his heels. "Okay, help me how?"

"I could tell you how to set up a business. I don't know exactly how things work here, but I can tell you the general principles."

"Why would I want to do that?"

"To free yourself to do more of the things you love."

Thorsten reached for her hand and pulled her to his side. "I already do what I love. I'm doing it right now." He kissed her and stroked a hand across her breast. Shannon melted into his touch. They lay back on the grass and enjoyed a brief exploration, like teenagers stealing one last grope before it was time to go home.

She wouldn't give up. "I've been thinking about it—"

"Apparently."

"—and here's what I see: You have this incredible store of photographs already. You take your twenty best —or maybe fifty, I don't know—and put together a portfolio."

"Uh-huh." He lifted her shirt and exposed her belly. He trailed his finger along the soft skin.

Shannon crossed her arms behind her head and closed her eyes. "A little higher..."

Thorsten obliged, cupping his hand beneath her breast and gently flicking his thumb across the nipple.

Shannon grabbed his hand. "Okay, enough. I can't think like a lawyer when you're doing that."

"Good."

Shannon squinted at him. "You don't want my help."

"In some things, but not that. I like what I do."

"Do you like the shrimp factory?"

"I do."

"Why?"

"Because I like the guys I work with, and I enjoy the work. It's good physical labor during winter."

"Don't the winters here seem long?"

"Yes, but that's good. There's time to do other things, like read, write—"

Shannon smiled. "Do you write?"

"Some."

"What do you write?"

"About nature, some of the places I've seen."

"Really?" Shannon asked. "Can I see it?"

"Sure, I suppose."

She threaded her fingers through his and pulled him on top of her. She laced her thigh over his and tempted him to do more.

"Should we keep hiking, or stay here?" he murmured between kisses.

"Stay here. I love you, Thorsten. I can't seem to get enough of you."


*I came here to propose,* Shannon had written playfully in the emergency shelter's logbook. It was the same lie she had told the group of kayakers when Thorsten's teasing put her on the spot.

She made love to him with a hunger that might have embarrassed her if they were anywhere but there. Somehow the emptiness, the solitude of the place freed her to live out a passion that would have worried her in closer quarters. She couldn't imagine giving herself to him so freely if they were in a hotel or at his place or hers. It was the vastness of Hornstrandir that set her loose, like a bird released from a cage. She abandoned any anxiety about their future, and resolved to simply live. To love. And to tell him so at every opportunity. Why not? She felt it, and he might as well know. She had never told a man so many times that she loved him. Thorsten heard it more in one day than Erik had heard it in a year.

It was a love that hurt sometimes because it was more than she knew what to do with. She could say "I love you" a thousand times, and still not reach the essence of what she meant. It was like trying to describe a foreign word using only a foreign language to do it. *"I love you" means "I love you," but can't you feel how hard I feel it? If you knew what it was like it would hurt you, too. It's too much for one person to hold.*

She amazed herself with this ability to separate thought from emotion. She knew their time would end—soon, in just a few days—but the facts had stopped intruding. For now, here in this vast cold place, she let her heart determine every move. *Should I kiss him now? Tell him I love him? Hold him, talk to him, dream with him? Is it time to make love? To share some part of my heart? Do I ask him now or wait until later?*

*Ask him now,* her heart responded, and the words were on her lips.

*Will you marry me?* She was sure he would—he had already said so.

*Ask him. Say it. See what can happen.*

"Thorsten..."

He gazed at her sleepily. "Hm?"

"I love you."

"I love you, too, Shannon."

"How much?"

"With all my heart."

She absorbed his answer, let it seep into her bones and trickle through her veins.

"What if I go away?" she asked.

"I'll still love you."

"Will you come after me?"

"Do you want me to?" he asked.

*No, because I don't want to leave in the first place. I want to stay here and marry you. I want to make children with you. I want to grow old and withered with you.*

She wove her fingers through his wavy hair and tasted a kiss from his mouth. "I want you to do whatever you want."

"All right," Thorsten answered sleepily, "I will."

Shannon waited, expecting to hear more. "What will you do?" she finally asked.

"It's a surprise," he answered.

THEY CAUGHT the ferry back on the afternoon of the sixth day. It carried them over storm-swept seas to the harbor of Ísafjördur, and deposited them back in the real world.

Shannon felt it as they walked from the dock toward the hotel. A dull buzz seemed to travel through her limbs, making each step feel leaden.

"What do you want to eat?" Thorsten asked her. "We could go to that restaurant. It's where I used to cook."

"Okay," she smiled wanly. "That sounds good."

She retrieved her luggage from the hotel and continued with Thorsten toward his apartment.

"Are you tired?" he asked.

"Not really."

"Feel all right?"

"Sure."

He stopped in the middle of the sidewalk. "Shannon, look at me."

She lifted her rheumy eyes.

"What's wrong?" he asked.

Shannon shook her head and continued on. Thorsten reached for her hand and she gave it to him, but she already knew the rest of her was pulling back.

*Nice try, Shan—really,* her belligerent conscience praised her. *You've had your fun. Now tell the nice man goodbye.*

"I should—" She paused and glanced back toward the hotel. "I forgot—they were going to make reservations for me—to get back to Annie's."

"I'll do that," Thorsten said. "Don't worry." He squeezed her hand. "Come on."

She soaked in his ancient bathtub while Thorsten downloaded photos from the trip. "There's a good one of you," he called to her. "When you were crossing the stream."

"Uh-huh—good," she replied with false cheeriness. It was all falling apart, and she had no one to blame but herself.

She changed into jeans and a sweater. She toweled off her hair and joined Thorsten in his gallery.

"You smell good," he said.

"Soap," she answered.

"Mmm. Much better than whale blubber." He leaned back in his chair and wrapped an arm around Shannon's waist. "Are you going to tell me now, or pretend that I don't know?"

"Know what?"

"That you're scared again."

He pulled her onto his lap. Shannon laid limp arms around his neck. "All right, I am. That's the truth."

Thorsten pointed to the computer screen. "See that?"

Somehow when she wasn't looking he had captured her smiling at some marvel of scenery. Her eyes shone and her expression was...joyous.

Shannon stared at that woman. Was that her just a few days ago? What had happened? Now her face felt heavy with the weight of reality. She couldn't imagine duplicating that smile.

"I want to show you something," Thorsten said.

He led her down the hall to one room she hadn't seen yet. It was the smallest of the bedrooms, made even smaller by the sloped ceiling. A futon mattress lay on the floor. Photographs covered every inch of the angled ceiling above Thorsten's bed.

"Lie here," he said.

Shannon complied. She leaned back against Thorsten's pillow and gazed up at the ceiling, only an arm's length away.

The first image that met her eye was one of her. He had taken it in Arizona. She wore a purple bandana over limp curls. Her face bore smudges of dirt mixed with sweat. And she was laughing.

She thought she might remember the moment—something Baby Michael had said that caused her to throw back her head and laugh with delight. It was a small moment, certainly not the best of the trip, but one she remembered nonetheless. And Thorsten had been there watching, recording.

There were other pictures. She didn't remember him taking any of them.

"Why?" she asked. "Why did you take these?"

"Because I already knew I would love you."

She turned to him. Her throat felt thick. "How?"

He pecked her lightly on the cheek. "I don't know. Come on, I'm hungry." He offered his hand and pulled her from the bed.

"Okay..." she answered, surprised at his abruptness.

"And can you bring your wallet?" he asked. "I'm out of money."

14

His strange behavior continued through dinner.

He talked incessantly to the staff at the restaurant, always in Icelandic, never including Shannon in the conversation. He introduced her as his "American friend," then never referred to her again as far as she could tell.

He ordered a bottle of wine and several courses, all without consulting Shannon about what she wanted. She picked at her food and stared glumly out the window while Thorsten enjoyed himself with his friends. He drank most of the wine himself, leaving her to nurse a single glass.

He leaned against her as they walked home, his gait unsteady.

"Was it a lot?" he asked.

"What?"

"Dinner. Expensive?"

She shrugged. "I guess."

He spotted someone he knew down the street. "Magnús!"

Thorsten confided to Shannon, "I used to sleep with his sister."

She stepped out of his lumbering hold and allowed him to meet his friend on his own. She followed several slow steps behind.

Thorsten and Magnús jabbered in Icelandic for several minutes while Shannon studied the books in a shop window. Finally Thorsten grabbed her hand and pulled her forward to meet his friend.

"This," Thorsten proclaimed sloppily, "is my new girlfriend. What's your name?" he asked Shannon, then laughed.

She ripped her hand away and smiled grimly. "I think I should go now."

"No, wait! Wait." Thorsten laughed. "I'm sorry, I'm a little drunk."

"I know."

Magnús asked something in Icelandic. Thorsten pursed his lips.

"He wants to know where I met you."

"At his brother's wedding," Shannon answered.

Magnús nodded and said something to Thorsten.

"*Nei*," Thorsten answered. "She's a virgin."

Shannon glared at her lover, then turned on her heel and headed back toward the hotel.

"Wait!" Thorsten called, laughing. "Wait. I'll be right there."

She strode on without looking back. When she reached the hotel she paused only briefly to see if he had followed her. He hadn't. She pushed through the door to the lobby and made arrangements for the night.

She lay awake for hours expecting to hear a knock or the phone ring any minute. Finally exhaustion overcame her and she fell asleep. She awakened the next morning still angry.

"Any messages?" she asked the woman at the desk.

"No, sorry."

Shannon wandered into the dining hall for a few slices of toast and several cups of coffee. She stared out the window at the morning's drizzle, wondering how and why her romance had taken such an ugly turn.

"Any messages?" she asked again before heading up to her room.

"No, sorry."

She sat on the edge of the bed and considered her options. All her luggage was at Thorsten's. She had her wallet, so could book passage back to Annie's. Should she cut bait and run? Or confront her former lover and retrieve her gear?

"Uh-oh," Annie said when she opened the door.

"Yeah," Shannon answered. Even hours later, her face still bore the disgusted frown of the morning.

"Hm. Should I ask?" Annie wanted to know.

"Ask away. I don't have any answers for you."


Her flight was leaving in three days. Still no word from Thorsten.

Shannon tried to distract herself while she spent the rest of her vacation with Annie and Kjartan, but the anger was too great to ignore.

"What did Kjartan say when you told him?" she asked Annie.

"Oh, he was so—"

"Can you believe they're brothers? How did Kjartan turn out so...so..."

"Nice?" Annie prompted.

"Exactly."

"Maybe Thorsten's just—"

"No," Shannon snapped. "I'm sorry I said anything. Let's not talk about him."

Still, she couldn't resist.

"Your brother is a bastard," Shannon told Kjartan their last afternoon of riding horses together.

Kjartan didn't answer.

"I don't understand him," Shannon tried.

"I don't, either."

As Shannon rode with Annie to the airport, the tears finally came. Thorsten hadn't tried to contact her once.

"I don't know what happened," Shannon told her cousin. Her eyes filled with tears. "I really thought he loved me."

"Do you love him?"

"I did. Yes."

"You realize I won our bet," Annie said. "Nanny Shannon."

Shannon smiled despite her sorrow. "Yeah. You were right. Too bad I didn't bet on how I'd feel right now."

Annie reached over and squeezed her cousin's hand. "I'm really sorry, Shan. I had no idea he was like this."

Shannon shrugged. "Lesson learned."

At the airport she nursed one last slim hope that he

would appear. She lingered over her goodbye, hoping at any moment she would spy Thorsten's tousle of brown hair and smooth athletic gait.

She boarded the plane with a heart so heavy she was sure it would sink to her shoes. As the plane lifted off she resolved to deaden herself to the pain. It was over. It had all been a massive mistake.

Back home she threw herself into work again, fighting her way up from the depths of misery. He didn't write, didn't call, and why would he? What clearer message could he have sent? For whatever reason, their brief affair had imploded. She knew she needed to forget him and move on.

Forgetting was the hardest part.

15

Stefán Kjartanson was born on March 8. His uncle Thorsten arrived a day later to congratulate the parents. Aunt Shannon was already there.

He wore his glasses. The eyes behind them looked at Shannon with what—sadness? tenderness?—she couldn't decide and didn't want to care. Shannon looked away.

"Here," Thorsten said to Annie, "I brought little Stefán a present." He handed her a wrapped gift. "And these are for you," he added, holding out a small vase filled with flowers.

"Thank you," Annie said. She accepted a peck on her cheek. "Here's your Uncle Thorsten," she said to the baby.

*Don't you dare trust him,* Shannon wanted to tell the child.

"How are you?" Thorsten asked.

Shannon waited to hear her cousin answer, then realized Thorsten was speaking to her.

"Me? I'm fine. Annie, can I take him for you?"

"Sure. Save my arm for later."

Just as Shannon accepted the bundle, Annie changed her mind. "Or, Thorsten," she said, "would you like to hold him?"

Shannon shot her cousin a significant look which went ignored.

"Yes, I would," Thorsten answered, "if Shannon doesn't mind."

"'Course not," she lied, "I can hold him all day." She transferred the baby to Thorsten's arms. Even that light contact with him was too much.

Annie unwrapped Thorsten's gift. She lifted her head and smiled. "Thorsten. Congratulations!"

He smiled shyly. "Thanks."

Annie held up the two books for Shannon to see, and translated the titles. "'*Trekkers' Guide to Hornstrandir* and *Kayaker's Guide to Breidafjördur*.' That's great, Thorsten—when did you do this?"

"Last year. Those are advance copies—they don't come out until a month."

Shannon noticed him looking at her. What did he want—her approval? *Forget it.*

"I'm going to get some coffee," Shannon announced. "Ann, you want anything?"

Annie was too busy smiling at her worthless brother-in-law. "Uh, no, thanks."

Thorsten said something to Annie in Icelandic, and she answered in the same.

*Great. They're all in it together.*

"Okay, I'm going now," she repeated.

Thorsten met her eyes. "See you."

She waited a good twenty, twenty-five minutes, hoping

Thorsten would have gone by the time she returned. No such luck.

Annie carted out the bad news right away. "Thorsten's going to stay in one of the guest cottages for a few days. I told him about the roof blowing off the stable, and he said he'll stay to help Kjartan."

*Great.* "Uh-huh," Shannon answered, her voice artificially high. "Okay, well, you should probably go now," she told Thorsten, holding out her arms for the baby. "Annie needs to rest."

Annie's raised eyebrow signaled she needed nothing of the kind, but Shannon was grateful her cousin went along. Thorsten handed over the baby.

"I'll see you later," Annie said. "Stefán and I should be getting out tomorrow."

"Good." Thorsten glanced at Shannon. "I'll see you later, too?"

*Not if I see you first.* "Uh-huh." She turned her back on him and carried Stefán to the window and pretended she needed to show him something outside in the parking lot.

When Thorsten was gone Annie said, "Well, that went well."

"He's staying?"

Annie shrugged. "I know it's hard, Shan, but try to be nice. It's just for a few days. Set a good example for your godson."

Shannon peered at the tiny boy in her arms. "Stefán, that was your uncle Thorsten. He's a terrible, terrible man and he lies."

Annie told her boy something in Icelandic.

"What's that?" Shannon asked.

"I explained that Uncle Thorsten isn't a bad man—he just doesn't know how to treat my cousin right."

"A terrible man," Shannon repeated to the baby, meaning it. "I'll tell you all about it when you're older."

AS HE WALKED AWAY from Annie's room, Thorsten's heart thundered in his chest. He had prepared for it, but seeing her was more than his aching heart could manage.

It was the hardest thing he had ever done, treating her that way on their last night together in Ísafjördur. He had hoped it would dissolve the one last barrier between them, but instead it had torn them apart.

He had watched the transformation, beginning on the ferry ride home. The woman who had been so loving, so open-hearted for the past few glorious days was slowly disappearing behind a wall of fear.

He saw it as they walked from the dock. Saw it in her slack mouth and that crease between her eyebrows. He hoped he was wrong—wanted to pretend that he was—but as the afternoon wore on he saw it all too clearly.

She was running again, after all that work. And he had very little time in which to bring her back.

He hoped that a continuous dose of tenderness would cajole her out of her fears. He invited her to his bedroom to show her the photos on his wall, hoping to persuade her that his feelings hadn't just materialized in the last few weeks, but had been there from the beginning, growing stronger all the time. It didn't work. She was falling fast into the well of disengagement, and he had to do something drastic.

So he turned into a royal bastard.

He intended it as shock treatment—something to jar her out of her passive stupor and force her to feel again—feel anything toward him, even anger. He pictured her screaming at him, telling him off. Then he would confront her with what he hoped was true: that she was looking for any excuse to flee from a love she knew was right. He had simply given her an easy escape route out. She could take it —leave angry with him and feel justified turning him away —or she could look inside her heart and admit that what she really wanted—what she *really* wanted—was exactly what he did: to make a life together, regardless of the obstacles.

But it hadn't happened like that at all. She had disappeared. She fled more quickly than he anticipated. He considered calling her, going after her, but then he realized he already had his answer. She didn't want his love after all. For whatever reason, she had decided it was too hard, and she wasn't willing to fight for it.

And that's when Thorsten's heart burst apart, and he was still looking for all the pieces.

"Hm. This is interesting," Annie said.

"What?"

Annie closed one book and flipped through the opening pages of the second. She looked up at her cousin. "'To Shannon.'"

"What to me?"

"Thorsten's books. He dedicated both of them to you."

Shannon traded Annie a baby for the books. She couldn't read any of the text, but her name on the page was unmistakable.

"That's what it says? 'To Shannon'?"

"What do you think that means?" Annie wondered.

Shannon handed back the books. "He said he wrote them last year. Must have forgotten to change them."

"I'm sure that's it," but Annie sounded less than convinced.

Shannon picked up the Hornstrandir book again. She fanned through the pages, scanning hundreds of photographs she remembered seeing on Thorsten's walls. The book was beautiful, she had to admit.

"Can you read all this?" she asked her cousin.

"Some of it, I'm sure. I'm still working on the language."

"You seemed to be fine talking to Thorsten." Shannon realized with embarrassment how snappish that had sounded.

Annie smiled indulgently. "He uses simple words with me. I still have trouble with normal conversation—it goes too fast."

"There's one thing I'd like to know." Shannon picked up the kayaking book. She looked at the index, then flipped to relevant page. "Read here."

Annie studied the words. "Gottfell Mountain…"

"Does it say anything about making a wish? Or about bringing someone along?"

Annie lifted her eyes. "Not just someone—you."

"What? Let me see." She scanned the page, looking for

her name. All she found were strange-looking letters and words that meant nothing to her. "Where?"

"Here. He says, 'I went with the woman I love.'"

Shannon chewed the inside of her cheek. "That could be someone else."

"Shan, he dedicated the book to you." Annie traced her finger along the rest of the paragraph. "'Legend says the mountain is magical.'"

"I know," Shannon interrupted. "Three rules. Climb before sundown—"

"Right. 'Don't look—'"

"—back. And take someone—"

Annie smiled as she read the words. "'Who holds a piece of your heart.' Very nice."

Shannon shrugged. She didn't want to feel nice, she wanted to feel angry—justifiably angry.

Annie continued to read. "'I took the woman I love...'" She paused. "That's 'love,' Shannon, not 'loved'—I know what past tense looks like in Icelandic."

"It's a typo."

"It's not. He says he took you there 'and made a wish that I hope the mountain will grant me one day. I have...'" Annie hesitated over this last word.

"Have what?" Shannon prompted.

Annie smiled. "'*Trú.*' It means faith."

## 16

The luscious scent of fish stew invaded her sanctuary. Shannon lay reading in the downstairs bedroom of Annie and Kjartan's house, only a few doors away from the kitchen. She had been hiding there all afternoon.

She was hungry. She hadn't eaten since breakfast. But unlike the Arctic fox that had invaded their camp on Hornstrandir, she would not be lured so easily. She would wait until Kjartan returned from his visit to hospital. At least then she would have a chaperon.

Not that she needed one, Shannon reasoned. No matter what Thorsten wrote, the fact remained he had dumped her, and not lightly, but hard.

She had had time over the last several months to consider the irony of it. Their parting had been as abrupt as hers from Erik. Gone without a trace. No, Shannon reminded herself, Thorsten still had a part of her—her backpacking gear and her luggage. A small price to pay for her dignity. He could sell them, for all she cared.

Reclining in the small guest bedroom, Shannon let her anger refuel itself. By winter last year she thought she had finally managed to bury it, but then Thanksgiving came and Christmas, and she couldn't help wishing...

Wishing what? That he was there with her? That she was with him in the darkness of an Icelandic December? No, just wishing she could understand everything that had happened. As with any new case dumped on her desk, she dissected every fact, played out every theory she could imagine, drew informed, intelligent conclusions and finally developed her strategy.

But Thorsten wasn't a case file, and the love she had felt for him—still did feel for him, if she cared to admit it, which she didn't any more—that love eluded her attempts to understand it. That love was a fact, as tangible as the numbers on a financial statement, as irrefutable as a sworn confession of guilt. What didn't make sense was the conclusion. If anyone had asked her last July to predict where her relationship with Thorsten would take her, Shannon would have bet on a bridal veil. If someone had stopped her as she waited for the ferry back from Horn-strandir and asked, "Excuse me, miss, is this the man you will marry?" Shannon would have answered an unqualified "yes."

Thorsten hummed in the kitchen and made her burn with frustration. How could he be so happy? Didn't he know she was just down the hall? Didn't he care that she hated him so much?

*No*, Shannon corrected herself, *you know that's not true.*

*Regretted, then. We regret him. We regret to inform you...*

A knock on her door. "Shannon?"

She bolted upright. "Yes?"

"I made dinner. Do you want some?"

"No, thanks." Polite, firm, mature.

*I wouldn't eat your food if it was—*

"Shan?" His voice softer now.

She hesitated. "Yeah?"

The door opened inward. He stood there in sweatpants and a long-sleeved T-shirt and wool socks. His hair was still damp from the shower. He wore his glasses. He had no right to look so good.

"What?" Shannon asked sternly. She sat on the edge of the bed with her finger marking her place in the book.

"Um..."

"I'm not hungry. Thanks." She pretended to read. He didn't leave.

"How have you been?" Thorsten asked.

This was too much. Her rage was too close to the surface. "How have I been? Great, Thorsten, just great. Thanks for the lovely send-off. I had a wonderful time. Do you still have my pack? Or are you keeping that as a memento? Some kind of token to prove I was there?"

He absorbed the barrage. Then he took a deep breath.

But Shannon wasn't ready to hear his answer. "And take my name out of your books. You don't have my permission. Is it anywhere else? Besides the dedication?"

Thorsten waited for the hostility to subside. He held her gaze until Shannon felt ashamed she had let him see her that way. He had no business knowing how deeply he affected her.

"I can't take it out," he finally answered. "The book is already at press."

Shannon shook her head in disgust. "I don't understand you at all."

The door to the house slammed shut. "Shannon?"

"In here," she shouted, her eyes steady on Thorsten's. If he wouldn't back down, neither would she. It was what she was trained for.

Kjartan joined Thorsten in the doorway. "Annie asked me to tell you there's more."

"More what?" Shannon asked.

"She said you'd understand." Kjartan looked at his brother and shrugged. "Is that dinner?"


The happy family of three sat at the long kitchen table and ate in utter silence.

Kjartan seemed content with it—he concentrated on his fish stew and processed whatever multiple pieces of information the farm had thrown at him that day. From what Shannon saw, there was always something to do—mend fences, tend the horses, maintain the equipment, manage the bookkeeping, repair whatever damage winter storms brought their way. A week ago a late-night blizzard had ripped the roof off one of the smaller stables. Kjartan had braved the leveling winds to usher the horses to safety, while Annie watched anxiously from inside the house. Annie confessed to Shannon what she worried about most after Kjartan's safety that night was whether the baby would decide it was his time to join them. She didn't relish the idea of braving the blizzard to drive to the hospital.

But the night Stefán was born was clear, and Shannon had accompanied her cousin in the back of the van while Kjartan drove. Shannon was grateful to have arrived in time. Her plane had only landed that morning.

"How's Annie?" Shannon asked Kjartan as he ladled more stew into his bowl.

"Good."

"And Stefán?"

"Good."

Kjartan wasn't trying to be difficult, Shannon knew, but sometimes holding a conversation with him felt like pushing a rock up a hill. To make matters worse, from the corner of her eye she caught Thorsten's amused smile. She ignored it and tried again.

"Did Annie sleep at all today?"

"*Já.* A few hours, she said."

"Good. That's good."

Thorsten stood to clear the table. "Are you finished?" he asked Shannon.

She nodded. His fingers brushed against hers as he accepted her bowl. A sliver of electricity ran through her arm. *Don't you dare,* she warned herself. *Not again.*

She pushed her chair back. "Well, I think I'll go to bed. See you in the morning," she told Kjartan.

"*Já.* See you."

She paused in the kitchen doorway. Thorsten's back was

to her as he washed off the dishes. "What time are you picking up Annie tomorrow?"

"Ten o'clock," Kjartan answered.

"I'll go with you, if you want."

"Sure."

She saw Thorsten shake his head. It irritated her more than it should have. "What?" she challenged him. "Thorsten, is there a problem?"

He turned and gazed at her with a familiarity she didn't like. "No, no problem."

"Fine." She turned and headed down the hall.

She felt him following, but refused to turn around. Her hand was on the knob when he stopped her.

"Can I talk to you?"

"No."

"No?"

"No." She twisted the knob and stepped into the room.

Thorsten glanced behind him, then entered after her. Softly he shut the door.

"I don't want you in here. Get out."

"Shannon, please stop this. I want to talk to you."

"I don't care what you want."

Thorsten's shoulders sagged in resignation. "Okay. I'm sorry."

They were words she had been waiting to hear, even though she knew they were out of context. "You're sorry? Sorry for what?"

"For disturbing you."

He exited the room and closed the door behind him.

It was like having a seed between her teeth.

She sat on the bed and fumed for several minutes, then gave in to her impulse. She stormed into the kitchen, hoping to find him there, hoping to confront him in front of his brother and make Thorsten explain exactly why he had treated her the way he had.

But he wasn't there.

Kjartan was, poring over some figures on a notepad.

"Where's your brother?"

"Went to bed."

Shannon tapped her socked foot against the floor. When she didn't leave, Kjartan looked up. "Do you need something?"

*Revenge. Satisfaction. A piece of his hide.*

"No, thanks." She stepped back into the hall. A left turn would take her to her room. A right would take her to the front door.

Shannon turned to the left.

ANOTHER DAY OF MURKY LIGHT. It suited Shannon's mood. She rose feeling achy and tired.

He hadn't come to her.

It was juvenile, she knew, this hope that Thorsten would chase her down, confront her, so she could scream at him and get it over with.

*He probably expected you to come to him. Fat chance!*

It was late—nearly 8:00. The winter's dark mornings made it hard for her to get up. Kjartan would be leaving soon, she guessed. Shannon pulled on jeans and a sweater and padded down the hall to the bathroom.

She brushed her teeth and splashed water on her face and hair, then combed her fingers through her curls. *Good enough—no one to impress here.*

She hadn't smelled his cooking, so Shannon didn't expect to see him when she stepped into the kitchen, but there he was.

"Good morning."

"Morning," she muttered. She moved straight to the cupboard and took down a mug, then kept her back to Thorsten while she lingered over getting her coffee.

"Where's Kjartan?" she asked.

"In the stables. He said to wake you at eight."

Shannon was grateful she had beat him to it. She took a sip of coffee and avoided looking at him. "Okay, well..."

"Do you want breakfast?"

"No. I'll catch something later." She slipped out of the kitchen and back to her room. Her stomach grumbled. *Traitor.*

She added a layer of long johns under her jeans and sweater, then headed for the hall. Like everyone else in the house, she had deposited her coat and boots by the door whenever she entered. Now she sat on the chair in the entryway and laced up one of her boots.

"Going to the hospital?" Thorsten asked. He leaned against the wall too close to her.

"Yep." Shannon kept her eyes on her work. She hated the buzzing in her veins as her nerves floated to the surface. Her heart raced, prepared for either fight or flight—she didn't at that moment know which. *Stop it, weakling. Get a grip.*

"Excuse me," she said, pushing his foot out of the way to

get to her second boot. *That felt good, didn't it? Next time push a little harder.*

Her reaction startled her. *Take it easy, killer. No bloodshed today.*

"What do you think Annie would like for lunch?" Thorsten asked. His voice was softer than it should have been under the circumstances. Couldn't he see she was angry with him?

"How should I know?" Shannon snapped. She stood and grabbed for the door.

A streak of maturity took hold. The truth was, she wanted Annie to enjoy a nice homecoming meal after two days of hospital food.

Shannon turned. "Okay, I'm sorry. That would be nice of you. She likes pizza. And spaghetti—something with sausage or beef, if you have it."

Thorsten nodded. "I'll see what I can get."

"Thank you." She shut the door before either one of them could say any more.

Positioned in the van beside Kjartan, Shannon asked, "How long is your brother staying?"

"I don't know, maybe until tomorrow."

*Good.*

For once Shannon was grateful Kjartan wasn't a talker. She spent the drive to the hospital staring out the window and mulling over thoughts as dark as the day.

Shannon's mood improved the moment she saw her cousin. "You ready? Where's my boy?"

"They're bringing him." Annie kissed her husband and

exchanged a few sentiments in Icelandic. Then she turned to Shannon. "Did you get my message?"

"Message? What—oh, that. Yeah. But I don't understand."

"Kjartan, can you go check on Stefán? I'm ready to get out of here." When they were alone, Annie removed one of Thorsten's books from her bag and flipped through the pages. "I saw it last night—let me try to find it again."

Shannon looked at the cover. It was the Hornstrandir book.

"Here," Annie said. "It's about the emergency shelters. It says, 'Hornstrandir is not for beginners, as many travelers have found. In addition to navigation and hiking skills, you must bring a special attitude with you. You must believe that what is worth having is worth pursuing to get.'"

Annie stopped.

"So?" Shannon said. "That's all true. It has nothing to do with me."

"This part does. 'If you visit the shelter at Hlöðuvík, look in the travelers' notebook...'" Shannon tensed. She remembered too well what she had written in that very book.

"'Read what people have written over the years,'" Annie continued. "'You will see who was prepared for Hornstrandir and who was not. Some people prepare for different things. One entry states that the person came to Hornstrandir to propose.'"

Shannon covered her face with her hands. "No..." She had already confessed that foolish spurt of optimism to Annie following her flight from Ísafjördur.

"Yes," Annie said, "and there's more. 'Hornstrandir will test you. It will test your will to succeed. It will test your ability to endure. And it can test your faith in the person with whom you go. I took the woman I love—'

"*Love*, Shannon," Annie emphasized. "'—and learned that she is a person who will never give up. It is why I have faith in her.'"

Shannon coughed. Something felt lodged in her throat. She gave her head a quick shake to make sure her eyes stayed clear. "I hate that man."

"No, you don't," Annie said, "and you know it."

"How could he write something like that? He knew I'd find out from you some day."

"Maybe that's the point."

"Well, forget it," Shannon said. "He had his chance—plenty of chances, in fact. It's been eight months, and he never made the slightest attempt to contact me. Forget it. He's leaving tomorrow and I can't wait to see him go."

"Are you sure about that?"

"Positive."

Annie closed the book. "Then I guess he was wrong. You do give up."

Shannon gaped at her cousin. "What do you suggest? How short is your memory? Do you understand how devastating that was to me?"

"Yes, but I also understand the reason why. It's because you love him, Shannon—*love*, present tense. You know it as well as I do."

"You're wrong. I—"

"Here she is," Kjartan cooed to his child. "Here's mama." He carried the baby to Annie. She nestled Stefán in her arms and shot a look at Shannon. "We'll talk more about it later."

"No, we won't."

"Shan," Annie laughed, "do you hear yourself? It's just me —remember? You and I get to talk about anything we want to. Those are the rules."

"But I don't want to."

"Then you should think about why that is."

If Kjartan hadn't been there, Shannon would have answered her cousin right then. *Because I'm through thinking about him and talking about him. It's over. I've moved on.*

Annie would have smiled at that. *"Oh, really?"*

## 17

Thorsten browned sausage in a pan already redolent with onions and garlic. He diced fresh tomatoes he had purchased for a warlord's ransom at the small grocery store half an hour away, and added them to a base of canned tomato sauce. He grated mozzarella cheese into a bowl and set it aside while he lined a baking pan with strips of cooked lasagna. The sauce bubbled about the same time the sausage was finished. Everything was going just as planned.

Cooking was always that way.

Love, that was more difficult. All the ingredients might be there, but if you added one too early or not enough of another one, the whole ensemble would fall apart.

But Thorsten believed in salvage. Scoop up the crumbs or the broken crust or the watery soufflé and make something else out of it that will be just as good, or even better.

He couldn't tell if he had made any progress at all.

Shannon still wouldn't look him in the eye. She seemed to be holding back a fury that he knew she needed to release, but that he didn't relish hearing. Sometimes an airing of grievances could be good for a relationship, but sometimes it only created fresh hurts that neither person could forget. Or forgive.

Thorsten removed from his shopping bag one last great luxury he had purchased. He pulled down a dusty vase from Kjartan's cupboard and washed it. Then he snipped off the ends from a stand of white roses and added them to the vase.

They could be for either woman. But he meant them for Shannon.

He puzzled over where to go next. Should he push her harder, force the confrontation he knew was brewing, or should he play it softer, more relaxed? Wait for her to come to him, or take the lead and actively pursue her? He had considered going to her room last night, but decided against it. Maybe she needed to get used to seeing him again before he sprung his affections on her. From the way she acted last night, he might have risked bodily harm.

Even that he could take, as long as it ended happily. And he needed it to end happily.

The last eight months had been misery. He knew he had handled her wrong, but didn't know what the next right step might be. Besides, he thought, she had made her own feelings clear by escaping when she could. He knew he shouldn't forget that.

But if there was any chance, any hope that the bond they

forged on Hornstrandir was strong enough after all to carry them through this difficulty, Thorsten wanted to know. He did not want to give up. It was one of the reasons he risked writing so personally in his guidebooks. The editor fought him on it—said it detracted from the tone of the work and made Thorsten look sentimental and foolish—but Thorsten didn't care. Some things were more important than what his fellow Icelanders thought of him.

He still had time to revise what he had written in time for the English translations to come out. By then he hoped to report better news to his readers.

From the moment she walked in the door Shannon felt that warm longing that comes from smelling something familiar. It wasn't the particular dish—she couldn't tell what it was beyond something Italian—but it was the feeling it evoked in her. Maybe it was the blend of spices he used or maybe it was her imagination, but the smell coming from the kitchen seemed to bear Thorsten's fingerprint and no other.

She missed him. So she went directly to her room.

"Wow, Thorsten, this is wonderful!" she heard Annie exclaim from the kitchen.

Shannon wondered how long she could hide without either starving or looking ridiculous in her cousin's eyes.

The latter became apparent immediately.

Annie entered without knocking. "Come out." It wasn't a suggestion, it was a command.

What could she do? Stamp her foot? Say, "Don't wanna!"?

"Be there in a second."

"Hurry," Annie said, "I don't know how much time Stefán will give me. I'd like to get a bite or two in before he wakes up."

Shannon washed her hands and made her way to the kitchen. They were all assembled, this Icelandic family of hers, with its newest member sleeping on Kjartan's shoulder.

Thorsten moved about the kitchen efficiently, filling plates with bread and salad and huge portions of lasagna. He set one down in front of her. She stared at it with what she hoped was detached admiration.

"These are pretty," Annie said, holding a rose to her nose. "Look, Shan."

"Uh-huh." She waited with eyes trained on her plate for the others to begin eating.

It was so...him. That unmatched quality of smooth texture and perfect flavor and touch of welcoming comfort.

"Mmm..." Annie moaned appreciatively. "Oh, Thorsten. Come stay any time."

Kjartan nodded in agreement. He carefully maneuvered his fork around Stefán lest he drip hot cheese on the baby.

"It's good," Shannon added quietly. Why not? They were civilized people, weren't they? She could throw him a small compliment without it meaning anything. Especially if she didn't look at him when she said it.

*You are the most immature...Stop it! Where's your spine? You have nothing to be ashamed of—you're here legitimately. He's the one who should feel uncomfortable, not you.*

Shannon sat up straighter and made a point of appearing unaffected.

She chatted with Annie about what the pediatrician had said, about what small marvels Stefán had carted out on his last day in the hospital, about anything but what was important.

"So you're leaving tomorrow?" Shannon asked Thorsten in her best lawyer voice.

"No...maybe...I don't know yet." He met the casual gaze she had leveled on him so defiantly. "It depends."

*I can guess on what.* She switched topics. "How's the roof?" she asked Kjartan.

"Nearly finished."

"Good. That's good."

The baby awoke. Annie stood and gathered him from her husband. "Guess I'm done for now," Annie said. "Can you save me some for later?"

"It will be here for dinner," Thorsten promised. "It's all I made for today."

"Believe me," Annie said, "it's better than what we ever have. You can serve it to me every meal if you want. Don't you think, Shan?"

It was hard to miss the mischievous glint in Annie's eye. Shannon smiled politely and said in her best imitation of a society girl, "Oh, yes. Can I come upstairs with you, Annie? I'd love to help." She stood without waiting for an answer and led the way.

When they were safe behind closed doors, Shannon rounded on her cousin.

"Listen, missy—"

"'Missy'?" Annie said. "This is serious."

Shannon stepped closer and said in an irritated whisper, "I'm serious, Ann. This isn't funny. You act like it's just a little lover's spat. That man dumped me. He abandoned me in a strange city and didn't care the slightest what happened to me after that. He loved me and left me. So all this cutesy little matchmaking isn't going to fly. I'm not interested."

Annie laid a towel on the bed and began changing Stefán's diaper.

"It's my sworn duty as someone who loves you," Annie said, "to save you from yourself. I know you love him. I also know he loves you. I'm sorry things ended the way they did last summer, but I think you need to look past that—"

"Look past it!" Shannon hissed. "Easy for you to say!"

"It is easy—I agree. But here's what I see: You have been living a pretty fruitless life these past many years."

"Thanks a lot."

"No, I'm serious. You've done great at your job, you have a beautiful house, you probably have some very nice friends, but your love life is a disaster."

Shannon sank onto the bed beside Stefán. She tickled her finger against the baby's hand.

"And…" Annie continued in the face of no objection, "ever since you met Thorsten at my wedding, I've had real hope that he was finally the one for you."

"You don't know anything about him."

"Yes, I do. I know he's a kind, intelligent, charming—"

"Right. Charming. That's where all the trouble began."

"—charming, handsome, loving man. He likes the same

things you do. He's everything you could want in a companion—"

"Except reliability. Trustworthiness. Fidelity."

"Fidelity?" Annie challenged. "Can I tell you something? I know a thing or two about Thorsten that you may not. He's not Erik, Shannon. He's not some man out plowing whatever field he can find—whoops, maybe that was too harsh."

"No, I think it probably wasn't. I'm sure Erik had lots of extracurricular activities."

"The point is, Thorsten isn't like that—not from what I've seen. I'm sure he's had plenty of opportunities these past eight months, but I doubt he's pursued a single one of them."

"How do you know?"

"Look at the evidence," Annie said. "That's what you like, isn't it? Some good, hard facts."

"What evidence?"

"His books, for one. Why would he dedicate them to you?"

"He probably wrote them months ago, and couldn't change them."

"When?" Annie asked. "When would he have written them? He didn't meet you until April. He saw you again in June and July. He must have decided after your trip here to dedicate them to you. Even if he decided to do that in April, he could have changed them after July. But he didn't. I'm betting he wrote those dedications after you left."

It made some sense the way Annie told it, but that wasn't enough.

"What else?" Shannon asked. "What other evidence?"

"You. You're my evidence. Have you slept with a single man since you came back from Iceland?"

"No, but that's me, Annie—not him. That's no evidence of what he's done."

"It is. Because I believe the two of you are more alike than you might want to admit right now. I think Thorsten has been acting the same way you have, moping around, feeling sad and probably a little angry."

This was too much. Shannon sat back up and prepared to make her case. "What does he have to feel angry about? You should have seen him! He was drunk and belligerent—"

"Belligerent? Really?"

"Okay, well maybe not," Shannon conceded, "but he was a pig that night—you should have seen him."

"That was one night, Shan."

"It was *the* night. Our last night together after such a great kayaking trip and then that wonderful time in Hornstrandir. That's what kills me! If you had seen what he was like on Hornstrandir, you would have been just as astonished as I was about how he acted when we got back."

"I think you're missing something," Annie said. "I don't know what, but I can't believe it's as simple as all that."

"It isn't simple at all—maybe you haven't been listening. It's very complicated and you're giving me a headache going over all of it again. Can we please talk about something else?"

Annie unbuttoned her shirt and let Stefán nurse. The gesture calmed both cousins. The topic changed of its own accord.

"He's so beautiful," Shannon said.

"He is," Annie answered. "I agree—maybe the mother isn't supposed to say that, but I'm amazed every time I look at him. I can't believe he came out of my body—that Kjartan and I made him together. It's a great system."

Shannon smiled. "That's one way of looking at it." She laid back down on the bed and rested her arm across her eyes. She sighed away any remaining tension. "Annie, I know you're trying to help—"

"Help myself, too, if you must know. We had that bet—remember? You were supposed to be Stefán's nanny for a year."

"Maybe next year. I'm swamped right now."

"Would you ever really do it? Come stay with me for a while—a long while?"

"I don't know. Maybe."

"Maybe if Thorsten were in the picture again," Annie said.

"Don't get your hopes up. He's good at dashing them."

"But you'll try?"

"No," Shannon answered. "Haven't you heard anything I said?"

Annie laid her sleeping baby next to Shannon, then reclined on the other side. She peered into her cousin's eyes. "Tell me the truth."

"Always."

"You wish you were still together."

"Of course," Shannon answered. "If it could be like it was on Hornstrandir."

"But even now—even after what happened. If you could find a way to be together you would. The truth."

Shannon sighed. "Okay, here's the truth: *If* he begged my forgiveness and *if* he explained himself so that I understood what that was all about last July and *if* I thought I could ever trust him again...then yes, I would love to be in love with him again."

"So that's all he has to do?"

Shannon chuckled wearily. "That's a tall order—especially the trust part. Speaking of which, this is cousin-cousin privilege, you know—on pain of death you are never allowed to reveal what I've said to you in confidence. I'm invoking the privilege. Everything we just talked about is private."

"I wouldn't say anything," Annie assured her.

"Not even to your husband."

"Not even to him. I promise." Annie stroked a finger across her baby's cheek. "But if Thorsten should ask me for advice—"

"No. Not a word. It's no good if he doesn't figure it out for himself."

"Okay, fine. But I have faith in him. I think he'll figure it out."

"Doubt it."

"Didn't he already buy you your favorite flowers? You think those roses were for me?"

Thorsten had a strategy now. He had thought about it all afternoon. He had broken through that tough outer crust once before, on Hornstrandir, and he would do it again.

What had worked before was anger. It had been real that

night on Hornstrandir, before the storm that destroyed Shannon's tent, but Thorsten thought he could duplicate the emotion.

When Shannon arrived last for dinner, instead of jumping up and serving her as he always had, he remained seated and ignored her. He ignored her for the next hour. He never looked her way, never addressed her, didn't smile at anything she said to Annie or Kjartan, didn't react in any way to her presence.

"Think I'll stay until next week," he told his brother. "I brought my work with me, so it's no problem. I'd like to help you get those fences in the south pasture mended. And anything else you need help with—I've got the time."

"*Já, takk*," Kjartan answered.

"Wonderful," Annie said. "I hate to seem selfish, but will you still cook?"

"Of course. It's nice to have someone like my cooking so much."

"It is good," Shannon agreed quietly.

He ignored even that.

When Kjartan headed for his office to work on the books and Annie answered her baby's call, Thorsten quickly gathered the dishes and carried them to the sink.

Shannon picked up a dishrag. "Here, I'll help."

"No, thanks," he answered. "You can go."

"I can go?" she repeated, as though he had just dismissed her as his servant.

"Yes. I know you have other things to do."

"Fine." Shannon retreated from the kitchen, leaving

Thorsten with no sense of satisfaction. This wasn't working, either. Tricks and games weren't the way.

He followed her down the hall and caught up with her as she reached her room.

"Shannon—"

She turned on him. "What?" Any shred of dinner's civility was gone.

Thorsten stared into her obstinate eyes. "Nothing," he answered. He turned back toward the kitchen.

"What, Thorsten, do you have something to say to me?"

"Yes, but maybe not now. Maybe not ever." He continued on his course, wondering whether anything would clear the air. Maybe it would be better if he left tomorrow after all. Maybe this whole attempt at reconciliation was a mistake.

He finished cleaning the kitchen and said goodnight to his brother. He paused in the entryway and considered whether to go to Shannon's room one more time. But he didn't have the words, and he didn't have the energy for another confrontation. Maybe he would try something else in the morning.

He shut the door behind him and stepped into the crisp dark night. He trudged up the footpath to his cottage. The air smelled of horse and snow and cold—so different from the scents of his seaside home. Maybe, he thought, he would be coming to the farm more often now that Kjartan and Annie had a child. Maybe he could forge a new connection with his sole remaining family. He liked the idea of being an uncle. He liked knowing there was more to his family now than just his brother and him.

Thorsten opened the cottage door and removed his

boots. He set water to boil on the small stove and plopped a tea bag in a cup. An hour or so of work would clear his mind, he decided, and take it off of his heart.

ONCE AGAIN SHANNON stood in the hallway. Once again she faced the decision whether to go left and return to her room or go right toward the front door.

Knowing she might be wrong, Shannon turned right.

## 18

---

Light filtered through the cottage window. She could
see the outline of Thorsten's head as he sat on the
futon sofa.

She waited outside the cottage long enough to feel the cold
seeping into her bones. She hadn't dressed warmly enough for
a nighttime vigil. She would have to press forward or retreat.

Shannon knocked on the door.

"Hello."

"Uh-huh," she answered, pressing past him into the
room. Papers and books lay strewn about the sofa and the
floor. A notebook and pen rested on top.

She removed her boots in deference to Icelandic custom,
but kept her coat on. Thorsten cleared away a spot on the
sofa. "Do you want to sit down?"

"No. Here's the thing: I decided I should have let you talk
to me yesterday when you came to my room. You seemed to

have something to say. So go ahead." She crossed her arms over her chest and kept her distance.

Thorsten leaned back on the sofa. "All I wanted to say was I hope you're okay."

"I'm not okay," she answered. "I'm very, very angry. I'm humiliated. I'm so mad I could spit."

He studied his hands and nodded. Silence gripped the room. Finally Thorsten lifted his eyes and asked, "What are you angry about?"

Shannon gaped in amazement. "What do you mean, what am I angry about? You left me, Thorsten—"

"No, you left me."

Again his ignorance—or feigned ignorance—brought her up short. "Thorsten, let's think about it. One minute I'm telling you I love you, and—"

"The next minute you're gone."

"Because you treated me like garbage."

"Because you wanted to go."

His answer hung in the air. Shannon shifted her weight to the other foot.

"I thought you loved me."

"I do, Shannon, with all of my heart."

This wasn't going at all as she had planned. Shannon leaned against the closest wall and regrouped.

"Let's go over it again," she began, hoping a little logic would get her back on track. "We came back from Horn-strandir. We went back to your apartment. I was going to spend the night."

Thorsten draped his arm over the back of the sofa. He

was too relaxed, Shannon thought with irritation. If she was keyed up, he should be, too.

She pointed at him. "Then you ruined everything."

"How did I ruin everything?"

"By ignoring me, by getting drunk, by—"

"Taking money from you?"

"Yes. And by treating me like some—some—"

"Why would I do that?" he asked her.

She threw up her hands in frustration. "Exactly! Explain yourself."

Was that a smile on his face? Of all the things—

"Shannon."

"What?"

He patted the sofa. "Come sit with me."

"No, Thorsten, I'm serious. I want to know what you have to say."

He removed his glasses once again and pressed his fingers against his eyes. She recognized it now as a stalling technique—she had techniques like that of her own. It was a way to seem calm and unaffected when all hell had just broken loose in the courtroom. When he was ready, he put the glasses on again.

"Shannon, I love you."

"You can say that, but it doesn't mean anything."

"It means everything. To me."

"Not to me."

But somehow—against her will and better judgment— she felt herself softening. Maybe it was her spent emotion or the length of the day or the fact that the sky had been gray since she woke up and she never felt fully awake.

She slid down the wall and sat on the floor. The wall heater warmed her corner. She wasn't in such a hurry anymore. In fact, it was nice to sit quietly.

To sit quietly in a room with Thorsten, no matter what he had done.

She still loved him. And she missed him. And she couldn't let him know either one.

She wrapped her arms around her knees and allowed her head to droop. She was unreasonably tired. A nap would feel good.

"Can I talk to you now?" Thorsten asked softly.

Shannon nodded.

Thorsten rose from the sofa and joined her against the wall. He pressed his leg against hers. It was a comforting gesture, and one that she welcomed. No matter how long they had been apart, his body still felt like a perfect match. Shannon moved her shoulder closer and let him take some of her weight.

"I didn't know what to do," Shannon confessed.

"When?"

"When we got back to Ísafjördur. I knew it would all end soon, and..."

"But it didn't have to."

She tilted her head to find his eyes. Then she gazed back at the floor. "Yes, it did."

He reached for her hand and threaded his fingers through hers. "Shannon, I'm so sorry. I didn't want it to end like that. I didn't want it to end at all. I still don't."

"Then why did you act that way?"

"It was stupid. I made a bad plan."

"Oh, you mean treat your girlfriend like crap? You think that's a bad plan?"

"I wasn't going to do it all night. You left before I could explain."

"You could have found me," Shannon said. "You knew where I would be."

"That was a bad plan, too. I messed up everything."

"Yes, you did."

"But you did, too," he said, not letting go of his argument. "You could have come back, but you didn't. You left without a word."

*Just like with Erik. But Erik deserved it.*

*Admit it—Thorsten didn't.*

Shannon sank against Thorsten in genuine weariness. All the fight had gone out of her. She leaned her head against Thorsten's shoulder and watched as he smoothed his thumb across her palm.

Without sensing that either of them had moved, she found her lips on his. And in her surprise she also discovered relief, and then comfort, and then the familiarity of touching someone who was as much a part of her as her own skin.

They didn't speak. There was no need. Words would only interfere with what was purely instinct. She held his face between her hands and gazed into his eyes, then closed her own and let the sensation carry her away.

For the past eight months there had been a hole in her heart, a tear too small for the human eye to detect, but one too large to ignore for more than a few hours at a time. Daily she mourned the loss of a love she believed in. She mourned that newborn, innocent part of herself that had allowed her to fall in love again and to throw herself into it so completely, only to be rejected in the end. She mourned the happiness she believed a life with Thorsten would bring. She had been ready, she thought, to take the final step and commit to a future unlike any she had imagined. But then it had all fallen apart.

Did she share some of the blame? She hadn't seen it before, or maybe she hadn't been willing to admit it, but now she could understand Thorsten's argument. She had left him. With good reason, she thought at the time, but ultimately she had been the one to leave without trying to work things out.

She tasted his breath as it mixed with her own. She drank from his lips with a hunger that had been building for so long. It was time, she thought, time to let go of that last imaginary handhold, and reach for the top of the climb with one last brave effort.

He guided her to her feet, then into the bedroom and onto its single bed. It was as wide a palette as Thorsten's sleeping bag had been, and there was comfort and familiarity in that, too.

She lifted his T-shirt over his head and kissed the flesh beneath. Thorsten began with her belly, softly stroking it, kissing it, then moved higher, slipping her bra above her breasts and welcoming them with a soft moan of pleasure and a mouth that knew what to do.

They stayed like that for half an hour, exploring the contours of each other's torsos from the waist up, stroking hands across backs, intertwining fingers and kissing mouths and pressing skin to skin in glorious rediscovery.

Shannon strayed first, dipping her hand beneath his waistband and gripping him with measured force. He breathed harder, suppressing a cry, and unzipped her pants to return the torment.

They stroked each other, relishing the wetness of anticipation and the discipline it took for neither of them to give in. Not yet. They had waited too long to hurry.

"I'm cold," Shannon whispered.

Thorsten repositioned them beneath the sheets.

"Too many clothes," Shannon murmured. She removed her jeans, but left her underwear on.

Thorsten groaned but smiled. He removed the rest of his clothes and lay naked beside Shannon, separated by only a thin piece of cloth.

Finally she let him go further. He pulled her underwear down her thighs, then slipped them past her toes.

"Are you sure?" Shannon asked. Her eyes were drowsy with arousal. She took hold of Thorsten and teased him against her moisture.

"Shannon, I'm—"

He released in her hand. She quickened her strokes and dipped him inside, relishing even that taste of him, knowing there would be other chances if she waited a while.

He buried his face against her neck. "I'm so sorry." He slid his hand between her thighs and prepared to bring her release of her own.

"No," she said, "not yet. Let it build. It'll be that much better next time. Go to sleep. I love you."

She had missed this part of him, the tender embrace, the soft kisses, the words of love before he drifted off to sleep.

He bathed her in all of those, and what she wanted most was the words.

"Shannon, I love you so much I can't bear it. You don't know how hard it's been not to see you. I can't believe you're here. I can't believe how much I love you."

She wanted to trust that he meant it. She wanted to forget the pain she had nursed over the past several months. She wanted to believe that this time, this love, was as real as any she would ever find, and that what her heart was telling her was true.

She wanted to know that this man, this one man, was finally the one she could give all of her love to, and know that he would hold it secure and treasure it and return it to her a hundredfold.

She combed her fingers through Thorsten's soft wavy hair and made a wish worthy of Gottfell Mountain:

*Don't let me be wrong. Don't let this be a mistake. Please, I want it to last.*

A few hours later she woke him.

"Come on," Shannon said. "My turn."


When she awoke the next morning she lay in bed alone. She strode naked into the front room.

"Mmm, that's nice," Thorsten murmured appreciatively, opening his arms. She leaned back against him on the sofa. He wrapped her in his limbs.

"What's all this?" Shannon asked, waving her hand over the books and papers lying all around.

"My translation. The publisher is paying me to translate my books into English. It's due next month."

"Can I ask you something?"

He kissed the top of her head. "Yes."

"When did you see what I wrote in that logbook? That day we were there?"

"No. I guided some trips in Hornstrandir last summer after you left. I saw it on one of those."

"Can I ask you something else?"

He kissed her head again. "Yes."

"What did you think? I mean, we had already—well, just tell me what you thought."

"I thought there was hope."

"Just because of that?"

"No, because of everything," he answered. He stroked the skin below Shannon's breasts. She rested her fingers on top of his hand and let him.

"Did you know I would come back?"

"Yes, because of Annie. Even before I knew she was pregnant, I knew you would come back some time to visit her."

"What were you going to do then?"

"What I did. Show up here and try to make things better."

Thorsten's hand moved lazily across her skin, creating anything but a lazy reaction in Shannon. She trapped his hand against her breast. "Don't do that unless you mean it."

"Maybe I mean it."

"Then prove it."

When they finally emerged from the cottage it was midday and Annie had been up for hours.

"Since about two o'clock this morning," Annie told them both as they sat drinking coffee with her. The baby was sleeping at the moment. Kjartan was out in the field.

"So," Annie ventured, "is it all right to say I'm happy to see you both so happy?"

Shannon lifted her eyebrow at her cousin in warning, but Thorsten answered, "Yes."

Annie grinned. "Good. Now can we get to something much more important? Thorsten, I ate the last of your lasagna this morning, but I'm still starving. Little Stefán eats like a sumo wrestler. I have to keep up."

Thorsten bounded from his chair. "Yes, absolutely. What would you like?" He scanned the contents of the refrigerator while Annie and Shannon shared a private glance.

Annie smiled and wiggled her eyebrows. Shannon rolled her eyes and whispered, "You're so immature."

"Do you love him?" Annie mouthed.

"Yes," Shannon mouthed back. She glanced up to find Thorsten observing the whole performance.

"What?" Shannon asked sternly.

"Eggs or porridge?"


The hard part was over, Thorsten thought, and now for the fine detail.

She loved him. She forgave him. Now how could they make this work?

"Stay," he asked her that night as they lounged in sleepy satisfaction.

"I can't."

"Why? Come back with me and stay awhile."

"I can't, Thorsten—really. I only have another week here, and I want to spend it with Annie. This was the only time I could take off. It's incredible—I just got my raise to ten weeks of vacation, and I can't seem to spend any of them. I have a trial next month and a slew of depositions to take before then. Then I have another trial in May. I don't know how it happened, but I'm buried in work this spring. I probably won't come up for air until June. Can you at least stay here until I leave next week?"

"Yes." *But what then?* Weren't they right back where they had been that last fine day on Hornstrandir? She was leaving, he was staying—they were no closer to making a life together.

"Can we talk about the future?" Thorsten asked her. "I want to know what happens next."

"Do you have a plan?"

"Maybe. I thought I could come see you in Minneapolis after I finish my translation. Then you can come back in the summer."

Shannon finished the thought. "And then you come to me, and I come to you...and how long do you think we can do that?"

"I don't know," Thorsten answered truthfully. "Maybe you have a plan."

"I do, but you won't like it."

She was right. He didn't.

## 19

Shannon wrestled her overstuffed document case into the house. She immediately kicked off her high heels and pulled off her panty hose. Just one more quick adjustment—taking off her bra—and she might be able to forget the tortures of the day.

She climbed the stairs to her bedroom and changed out of her linen suit. She pulled on light cotton pants, unhitched what she used to think of as her lucky litigation bra, and slipped into an oversized T-shirt.

At times like these she would have loved to come home to a friendly face. But that was just the way it was.

*What a disaster.* A client who self-destructed on the stand, an opposing attorney who accused Shannon of misleading the court, a jury that seemed predisposed to hating everything Shannon said and did—on days like this she wished she worked with animals. Or flowers or food—anything but people.

Food. Funny how the slightest innocent thought could bring her right back to images of Thorsten. She pictured him in his tiny kitchen assembling some tongue-pleasing delicacy like ginger cookies or chocolate mousse or something he invented on the spot after asking if she wanted crunchy or smooth, salty or sweet. One night when they were still together at Annie and Kjartan's farm, Thorsten had unveiled a new treat: praline ice cream with slivers of fresh ginger and salty peanuts on top and caramel sauce on the side.

"Now I really love you," Shannon had declared in front of them all. "Just imagine what Baby Michael would say right now. He'd go down on one knee."

"I'd like it better if you would," Thorsten had answered pointedly.

"I'm not that liberated."

Oh, to have another night like that now, in the midst of this war. To come home to the man she loved and spill out the details of her day—or not—maybe that would be better. *Yes, just disappear into his embrace and forget everything. Let him spoon some rich, thick sauce into my mouth, then kiss him until he drops the spoon, then eat first to keep up my strength, then upstairs for the night...*

Instead she would be spending the night reading over depositions to prepare for the next day's atrocities. She wanted to think the trial couldn't get any worse, but that was probably too optimistic. The best that could be said for it was that it would be over soon.

And then. "Then" was what she lived for. Just sixteen more days. If she could hold on until then, this would all go away. She would be locked in his arms for weeks. *Weeks. Hallelujah.*

When Shannon first explained her plan to Annie a few months ago, her cousin had had the bad manners to remind Shannon of something she had said before. It was when they were talking about Thorsten the previous April, after the backpacking trip in Arizona. Shannon had questioned whether a relationship with Thorsten could ever work, and Annie told her to wait and see.

"I'm not a wait-and-see kind of girl," Shannon had proclaimed. "I like to know where I stand."

And here she was proposing just such a plan to Thorsten.

He reacted the way she had.

"No. That's not good enough," he said. "I love you and I want a life with you."

"I can't right now—how can I? It's not realistic."

"When will it be realistic?"

"I don't know," Shannon answered. "Let's just wait and see."

The months since then had crawled by at an agonizingly slow pace. They sent e-mails, spoke on the phone, tried to hear in each other's voices that same intensity of emotion they felt when they were together, but there was no question a long-distance romance was the pits.

What she wanted was the luxury of time—endless time with him. To wake in his bed, to putter through the day, to spend time outdoors with him or cozy inside with him, but generally the key was *with him.* Not without—she had tried that and didn't care for it at all.

Her brothers were less than sympathetic.

"You're an idiot," Michael declared. "I wish I was there right now so I could pinch you."

"Shan," her middle brother Will argued, "how many guys like that are you ever going to meet? I didn't get to know him as well as Chris and Michael, but from what I hear..."

And Chris, weighing in with, "You're what now—thirty-three? Tick, tock, Shan—let's get those monkeys in the oven."

"I think it's 'buns,'" she corrected.

"Geez, spare me the details. Grab whatever you want on him, but let's get this going."

Annie was more circumspect. "I'm already ahead of you in the baby game. If you don't want my boy beating up yours, you'd better hurry up."

All of which did nothing to answer the lingering question in Shannon's heart: Could she make it work this time? Excuses aside—matters of geography and employment and other inconsequentials—could she really make a marriage that lasted this time? Was she the right woman for this man? Was he for her?

He was the right man for her—she knew that. And in her private moments of self-evaluation, she admitted to herself she was the right mate for him.

*So what's the problem, Shan? Why haven't you closed the deal?*

She couldn't answer that. Or maybe she just didn't want to. Maybe she wasn't ready.

*Maybe, maybe, maybe...*

Before settling down for her nighttime reading, Shannon glanced at the calendar for the twentieth time that day.

Two and a half more weeks. Barely any time at all.

Then she and Thorsten would see.

WHEN SHANNON first suggested they not see each other until June, Thorsten objected.

"I can come to Minneapolis," he said. "In late April. Why wait until June when we can see each other earlier?"

"My life will be crazy. I have nothing but work between now and the summer. It won't be any fun."

"We'll make it fun," he answered, supplying a demonstration.

Shannon gently removed his hands. "Besides, I think we should wait and see."

"Wait and see what?"

"How we feel by then."

"I know how I will feel," Thorsten said. "Maybe you're the one who doesn't."

"Please. It's only a few months. Then I promise I'll come stay for a long time. They owe me that at work. I'll arrange it so I can stay through July."

"August," Thorsten negotiated.

"I don't know. Let's wait and see."

Now as the time approached he found himself thinking of it with sweaty palms. This had to work. He knew he might have only one chance to get it right. The plans were made, the details arranged—now all he needed was for Shannon to play her part. It was risky—she might not like it —but Thorsten was a man accustomed to risk.

He was also, he thought, becoming accustomed to the

way Shannon's mind worked. He hoped he had read her right. If not, it could be a short visit.

"I won't be there when you get in," Thorsten told her in a phone call a few days before her arrival. "I have to guide a group."

Shannon tried to disguise the disappointment in her voice. "This early in the season?"

"They want to be on Hornstrandir for summer solstice on the twenty-first. Can you meet me?"

"With the group? I don't know…"

"I'd like to spend solstice with you," he said. "It's very special. You can come over on the ferry on the seventeenth —that's Iceland's National Day, did you know? When we declared independence from Denmark."

"Will there be hot dogs and fireworks?" Shannon asked.

"Fireworks, yes, but only if we share a tent."

"I don't think your customers want to hear us mate—remember what Halldor said."

"We'll sneak away. I have it all planned. Don't worry—just come."

They made arrangements for her to get his key from a neighbor. Her backpacking gear was still in his apartment.

"I bought you a new sleeping bag," Thorsten said, "one that zips into mine."

"Did you buy me a new tent?" She smiled at familiar sound of the one Icelandic curse he had taught her.

Just two more days. Her nerves buzzed with anticipation.

·  ·  ·

THORSTEN MET HER ON SHORE, his smile as wide as the sea. Shannon threw herself into his arms and pressed her face against his neck to drink in the smell of him. Other hikers disembarked from the inflatable boat and milled about on the sand gathering their gear while Thorsten and Shannon continued to embrace.

"You should have let me come in April," Thorsten chided.

"I know."

The day was clear, the air crisp. A bearable wind swept along the shore. Shannon reached for her backpack, but Thorsten beat her to it.

"I'll carry it," he said. "Mine is at the campsite."

"I can carry it," she argued, grabbing for the strap.

Thorsten leaned over and whispered, "I know you can, my love, but I want you to conserve your energy. I plan to keep you up all night."

Shannon couldn't resist that seductive smile. She helped Thorsten adjust the straps for his longer torso then set off down the shore with him, walking hand in hand as long as the trail would allow.

"How many in the group?" she asked.

"Just three, all men."

"And they know I'm coming?"

"They're looking forward to it," Thorsten answered.

"What's for dinner tonight?"

"Is that all you think about?"

"Of course. Did you think I came here for you?"

Thorsten ticked off the list: clam chowder, seafood pasta, pan-fried bread, chocolate raspberry pudding.

"You cook better for them than you did for me," Shannon complained.

"They're paying me to."

The campsite was a few miles inland, not far from where Shannon and Thorsten had stopped for soup their first night there. Shannon wondered if the same fox might visit. This time she would hold perfectly still in hopes it would linger longer.

As they ascended the slope she saw two tents in the distance. "Is that you?"

"Yes."

"Only two tents? Where will you and I sleep?"

"Don't worry. I took care of that."

As they drew closer Shannon saw one of the men emerge from his tent. He lifted his hand above his eyes and gazed down the hill at them. Something in his stance, maybe his way of moving, caught Shannon's attention. She squinted and tried to make him out.

Soon the other two joined him and then she knew.

Shannon broke into a run. "Boys!"


So far, so good, Thorsten thought. She was as happy as he had ever seen her. She had a particular laugh that he only heard when she was around her brothers. It was deeper and more musical. It seemed to travel from her toes out through her curls. Seeing her like this—so relaxed and thoroughly content—was reward enough for all the work that had gone into planning the surprise. He hoped his other surprise would turn out so well.

"Did I tell you?" Michael said to Will. "See what you missed?"

Will downed another heaping sporkful of pasta. "Not bad," he agreed, "but I still think my peanut butter supreme was a great meal."

The other siblings groaned.

"Ugh! That was the worst!" Shannon said.

"I don't think he meant for that hair to get in there," Chris replied.

"It wasn't the hair, it was the tuna," Shannon informed him. She turned to Thorsten. "Would you ever pair peanut butter with tuna?" She didn't wait for an answer, but continued berating her brother. "And the dried cabbage you sprinkled on top—that was disgusting. Rancid, wilted—"

Will shrugged indifferently. "You ate it."

Complaints flew then, each of them reminding the others of past offenses in camp cooking—burned meals, insufficient quantities, the crunch of dirt in what should have been a smooth noodle dish.

"There was grasshopper in mine," Shannon said.

"Hey," Michael defended, "prote."

"Prote?" Thorsten asked.

"Protein," came the answer from multiple lips.

He knew they hadn't seen each other for over a year, since Annie's wedding. Thorsten settled back into his camp chair and let the siblings talk. He joined in when he had anything to add, but otherwise he was perfectly content to sit quietly and observe the woman he loved share her heart with the other men she loved. He felt no jealousy—not even envy anymore. He saw now that what she felt for them was separate from the love she offered Thorsten. That love was passionate and nearly whole in its own way. All it lacked was a sense of completion—that last span of commitment that would close the circle.

Near midnight the conversation began to soften. Fewer words, less energy.

Thorsten heated a pot of water and poured hot chocolate for everyone. He added two thin pretzel sticks to each.

"A toast to my country," Thorsten said. "*Skál.*"

"*Skál,*" they repeated.

"I couldn't figure out what you were saying the first few times you said that at the rehearsal dinner," Chris confessed. "I thought you just had a bad accent."

"I do."

Shannon laced her arm through Thorsten's and pulled herself closer. "You want to know what I thought?"

Her youngest brother rolled his eyes. "No. This is family hour, Shan."

Shannon was undeterred. "I thought he was a smart ass—just like my brothers."

"Women always marry their brothers," Will opined. "Men marry their mothers."

"Uh-oh," Michael answered.

"Where is mom these days?" Shannon asked. "Wasn't she talking about going on a cruise?"

"More like a booze," Chris grumbled. "She's off the wagon again. She probably got on the wrong ship and is headed toward Antarctica on a Russian icebreaker as we speak."

The mood of the group declined. Soon the late hour

seized control, and one by one the brothers drifted off to bed.

"You coming, Thorsten?" Michael asked mischievously.

"No, I think I'll sleep someplace else tonight."

As soon as they were alone Shannon whispered, "Where are we sleeping?"

Thorsten shouldered her pack. "Come with me. I'll show you."

They hiked for twenty minutes, to the bank of a noisy river. Several waterfalls dropped into one another, churning the cold water.

Thorsten's green tent stood a short distance from the bank. An Icelandic flag flew from one of its poles.

"You're very patriotic," Shannon commented.

Thorsten's answer was sincere. "I love my country."

He set Shannon's pack next to his in the vestibule and unzipped the tent. He let Shannon enter first.

"What's all this?" she asked.

"Get in. I want to tell you a story."

# 20

"I lived with a family once that had a father who worked for archaeologists," Thorsten began. "He did the heavy labor at the excavation sites—hauling off the dirt, moving rocks, loading skeletons and artifacts into crates. The group he worked for was very successful—they found many old Viking homesites. This man—his name was Pétur—he would bring home photographs sometimes to show us what they uncovered. And sometimes he brought home little artifacts they had found. He claimed the archaeologists said he could keep them, but I doubt that was true. But I liked him because sometimes he gave some of them to us children."

"You and Kjartan?"

"No, Kjartan was with another family. I stayed with these people and their two boys." Thorsten lifted an ivory triangle from the top of his sleeping bag. "Pétur said this was a shark tooth one of the Vikings wore on a necklace. And this was a scrap of boot taken from one of the graves.

"And that was what interested me most," Thorsten said, "the graves."

"Ooh, why?"

"Because you could see what a man valued. Sometimes the grave mounds were huge—that meant a man was buried with his favorite horse. His friends or family would kill it so the man's soul could ride it in the afterlife. Sometimes there were whole families buried together, or mothers with their babies—life was very hard then, and there was a lot of sickness."

"So at least the people were dead before they were buried—right? It wasn't like with the horses."

"No, I don't think so." Thorsten held up a small golden amulet in the shape of a cross, with one end forming a dragon's head. "I think it was very bad to take this one. I've always thought I should leave it at a museum, but then I never do."

"Why not? What is it?"

"Thor's hammer," he answered, wrapping his fingers around the dragon head handle to demonstrate. "Thor was a god the Vikings used to worship. Then they converted to Christianity, so they kept the idea of his hammer but made it into a cross. I've always kept it because it was the last thing Pétur ever gave me before he died. But I should give it to a museum—it isn't right to keep it."

"How did Pétur die?"

"In a truck accident. He had been drinking, and..." Thorsten shrugged. "His wife couldn't keep me any more after that, so I had to go someplace else."

Shannon clasped his hand. "I'm so sorry." She had heard

portions of his childhood over time, but there always seemed to be more—more hardship, more heartache—than she imagined. "How old were you?"

"Old enough. I was all right." Thorsten cleared his throat. "But this," he said, holding up a tattered photograph, "was the thing that impressed me most of all."

Shannon studied the photo. It had been taken at the edge of a gravesite. Two skeletons lay side by side within.

"Pétur told me this was his favorite grave, and it's mine, too. This is a husband and wife."

They seemed to be lying on their sides, their knees drawn up, their bony fingers entwined in each other's.

"In all the other graves the couple lay on their backs with their arms at their sides or maybe crossed over their chests. But this one—Pétur said the family must have known the husband and wife loved each other so much they wanted to go into the afterlife looking at one another and holding each other's hands."

Thorsten paused. He cleared his throat again.

"Pétur told me they wore matching rings. He described them to me—strips of gold woven together. He said it looked like Brunhilda's braids."

Thorsten lifted his eyes to Shannon's. "I don't know if I got it right," he said softly, "but I tried." He reached inside his sleeping bag and retrieved a small box. He lifted the lid. "I want to go through my life looking at you and holding your hand." He removed the ring and placed it in her palm. "Please, Shannon, will you marry me?"

Tears streamed down both of their cheeks. Shannon swept her finger beneath Thorsten's eye and added his tear to her own. She kissed his salty lips and wrapped him in an embrace.

"I love you," Shannon whispered. "I don't want anyone but you."

Thorsten pulled back. "What does that mean?"

Shannon slipped the ring on her finger. She smiled. "How did you know my size?"

"Annie told me. What does this mean? Tell me yes or no."

"Thorsten, I'll marry you right now."

WHEN THEY RETURNED to camp in the morning, the brothers were already up drinking coffee.

"We're starving," Michael told his sister. "Did you have to keep him so long?"

"That's right, Baby Michael, because everything is about you."

"No, not everything. I recognize some things are about you."

"Like what?"

"You think we just came here to backpack?" He turned to Thorsten. "Is there going to be a wedding or not?"

"ARE you sure you want Stefán to hold them?" Annie asked. "He doesn't have great control over his hands yet."

"I'm sure."

As if to prove his mother's reservations, the baby flapped his arms in the air.

"I can just see the rings flying," Annie said.

"He'll do fine." Shannon rubbed her nose against her godson's cheek. "Won't you, Stefán?"

"I'm surprised you aren't mad at all this," Annie said.

Shannon laughed. "You mean the fact that my brothers came here expecting a wedding, and you already had my wedding dress picked out and Thorsten had rings made—why should any of that bother me?"

Annie scrutinized her cousin. "Are you being sarcastic?"

"No," Shannon said with a smile, "I am not. I love that the details are taken care of. I don't have to lift a finger. I just show up and say my lines—it's just like being a groom."

Annie slipped the lavender dress over Shannon's head. "I hope you like this all right."

"It's beautiful."

"I saw it in Reykjavík, and—"

"It's perfect." She smoothed the fabric over her hips. The hem reached just below her knees. She opened a fresh package of panty hose and pulled them on. Then she slipped into her shoes—lavender pumps in the size Annie and Shannon shared.

"Too much?" Annie asked. "It's a lot of purple."

"Frankly, I don't care what I wear. The dress is beautiful and the shoes, too, but I would have done this in my grungy backpacking clothes if I had to."

"That anxious, are we?"

"You might say that."

Annie eyed her suspiciously. "Why? Is there something I should know?"

"Like am I pregnant? No, but the truth is I wish I were. I haven't been on birth control since I left here in March."

Shannon pulled her bag onto the bed and fished inside. She pulled out a small manila envelope. "Look."

Annie opened the clasp and poured out the contents: A man's platinum ring.

"I was going to propose myself," Shannon said. "I decided I was acting like a complete idiot."

"And when did you have this brilliant epiphany?"

"One night when I came home from an awful day of trial. I sat there trying to read through a stack of depositions and decided that trying to get money for that client was the biggest waste of my life. Thorsten had offered to come see me in Minneapolis and I told him no because I had too much work. It was a terrible decision—the kind I've been used to making for too long now. I decided that when I saw him again I would start over—restructure my life, and for once decide what I wanted first. And what I wanted was him—rings, certificate, joint property or whatever they have here."

Annie nodded in smiling approval. "The transformative powers of the Icelandic man."

"I don't know about that, but I'll give Thorsten credit— he hung in there. He certainly worked the problem."

"And that problem was you?"

Shannon lifted her ring bearer from the bed. "Cousin-cousin privilege? Yes, I admit it."

Annie draped a receiving blanket over Shannon's shoulder. "Stefán, if you spit up on that pretty dress Mommy will be very mad."

"Don't listen to her," Shannon murmured. "You and I are a team."

As predicted, the exultant ring bearer threw one ring into the grass before being divested of the other. In keeping with ancient Viking tradition, the brothers of the bride demanded the *brúdkaup*—the purchase of the bride—in exchange for kayaking lessons. The ceremony was celebrated with a feast cooked by the groom himself. Wine was poured, hearts were opened, many tears were shed.

As they walked arm in arm from the main house to the cottage, the new bride looked to her husband.

"I have a confession to make."

"Oh, no."

Shannon smiled. "It's not bad. I'll show you."

They entered the bridal suite—the same summer cottage where Thorsten had stayed before, but this time bearing a new double bed purchased by the owner.

"I know how it is," Annie had told her cousin upon presenting it. "Kjartan and I have fallen off a few twin beds in our time."

Shannon retrieved her envelope and slid the ring into Thorsten's palm.

"What's this?"

"My proposal."

"Too late. I already have a wife."

But Shannon wanted to be serious. "Remember what you wrote in your book? That you had faith in me? At first I didn't want to hear it, but I've thought about it a lot since then. I think that's the sweetest thing anyone has ever said about me, and I wanted to prove you right."

She slipped the ring onto his right finger. "So maybe

you'll wear this one, too, so you'll always know how much I meant it."

"Come here," Thorsten said, leading her to the bedroom. They kicked off their shoes and lay side by side in their wedding clothes, fingers intertwined. Thorsten gazed into his wife's gray-green eyes. "This is all I ever wanted," he said, "from the minute I saw you."

"This is all? Then I have another confession to make."

"Okay," he laughed.

"I probably should have told you before, but...I stopped taking birth control. I was hoping—"

"Then we should get to work."

## 21

Thorá Thorstendóttir and Pétur Thorstenson were born March 17 in a Minneapolis hospital. Their uncle Kjartan, Aunt Annie, and cousin Stefán arrived a few days later. The twins' uncles Chris and Will and Michael were already there.

"You're so competitive," Annie complained as she lowered her pregnant body into a chair. "You had to have two children before I did."

"Who knows," Shannon said, "maybe you'll have little Óskar while you're here. Wouldn't that be fun?"

Annie smiled. "Actually, it would. We could set up a maternity ward in your house and I can enjoy Thorsten's cooking for a while."

"Let's ask the doctor," Shannon whispered conspiratorially. "Maybe he can give you something."

Thorsten stood in the doorway. "Ready? Your brothers have the car." He helped Shannon into the hospital's wheelchair and pushed her through the door.

"Aren't we forgetting a few babies?"

"Your brothers have them. How long are they staying?"


It was a feast reminiscent of the wedding. The menu was different—at Shannon's request, Mexican food this time—but the guests were the same, with two squalling additions. Shannon sat at the head of the table and took it all in.

Kjartan holding his sleeping son against his shoulder. Thorsten cradling one baby, Chris the other. Will and Michael trading one-liners while they waited for their turn with the twins.

"When did the boys get so paternal?" Shannon murmured to her cousin.

"Which ones? Your brothers or our husbands?"

"Oh, I knew Thorsten had it in him—I could see it from how he was with Stefán. And obviously Kjartan loves fatherhood—I've never heard him talk as much as he does to that boy. But what's with my brothers?"

"It must be time," Annie said. "Maybe they're finally ready to grow up."

"Never."

"Let's hope not," Annie agreed.

"I have a toast to make," Thorsten announced.

"*Skál!*" Will replied in readiness.

"No, a different toast." Thorsten stood, still holding baby Pétur, and lifted his glass. "It is a tradition in Iceland for the father of a new baby to give the mother a present."

"It is?" Shannon asked Annie.

"It is," her cousin confirmed.

"My first present is a toast to my beautiful, sexy—"

"Keep it clean," Michael warned.

"—smart, brave, strong, wise, hard-working, fun, kind—"

"I like this," Shannon said.

"—wonderful, exceptional, beautiful, wonderful wife." Thorsten raised his glass. "To Shannon."

"To Shannon!" the room echoed.

"The second gift—because there are two babies—is something I hope you will like." He reached beneath his chair and retrieved an envelope. He handed it to Shannon.

The document was entirely in Icelandic. Although Shannon had been working on the language, she was still in its elementary stages.

"Let me see," said Annie. She read for a moment, then her face broke into a smile. She lifted her eyes to Thorsten. "Really?"

"Really."

Annie handed the paper to her husband.

Kjartan translated for the group.

"It's about *Takk Fiskurs*," Kjartan said. "It's a restaurant my friends own—it's near our farm. They're moving to Reykjavík and want to sell. This paper says Thorsten has offered to buy."

"A restaurant?" Shannon asked. "But I thought we were going to live in Iceland only part of the year."

"We can open it for summer only," Thorsten replied. "There aren't many customers in winter."

"What about your guiding?" Shannon asked.

"I'd rather be with you and the children."

"What about your books, and your photography?"

"I'll still take photos. And I'll have winters here to write while you work."

She was having trouble hiding her smile. "Are you serious? You're really going to do this?"

"*We* are—if you want that. I found a house near Annie and Kjartan. It needs work, but—"

Shannon silenced her husband with a kiss. Baby Pétur objected loudly.

"Here, I'll take him," Annie offered, whisking the child from Thorsten's arms. Soon Thorá added her own voice to her brother's.

The room rang with laughter and chatter and newborn cries. Shannon sat in the midst of it all, loving the comfort it brought her.

She motioned for her husband to come closer. "Is this what you had in mind when you married me? A big loud family like this?"

"You're my family," he answered. "That's all I need to know."

# ABOUT THE AUTHOR

Robin Brande is an award-winning author, former trial attorney, black belt in martial arts, Reiki Master, and wilderness medic. Her outdoor adventures range from the Rocky Mountains to the Alps to Iceland.

She writes in multiple genres, including mystery, adventure, fantasy, science fiction, young adult, romance, and self-help.

*For more information:*
https://robinbrande.com/

**For information about new releases, along with special discounts on books and merchandise, subscribe to the Robin Brande newsletter: https://robinbrande.com/ pages/subscribe.**